Fairies, Robots and Unicorns—Oh My!
A Collection of Funny Short Stories

SARINA DORIE

ISBN: 1519557183
ISBN-13: 978-1519557186

DEDICATION

Dedicated to my brother, Dwayne. I can probably thank you—or blame you—for the development of my sense of humor.

CONTENTS

ACKNOWLEDGMENTS

I appreciate all the feedback from Wordos, my critique group, and that of my previous critique groups who inspired me to keep going and assisted me in knowing when to stop. Without these wonderful writers, I would not have made many of my short story sales, and the stories in this collection would not be what they are today.

Five Tips to Slay a Unicorn

Whether you are on a royal hunt, you are a sorcerer in need of a unicorn's magical horn, or are simply fed up with stallions carrying off all the fair maidens, be aware that mythical beasts can be cunning, dangerous and deadly foes. Do not be fooled by the beauty and elegance of these creatures, nor their air of innocence and purity encouraged by the princess community. They are in fact depraved and horny beasts who breed like rabbits; hence the reason they have overpopulated the forests and now run amuck in small villages, consuming crops and terrorizing the countryside. They have their pick of the best maidens and use magic to seduce them. Worst of all, they trample over the dignity of the common man.

There is a plague of unicorns upon our land and all must do their part in ridding our kingdom of them. Follow these easy tips if you wish to join the battle against the horned ones and wipe them out of existence:

1. You need a fair maiden. Contrary to popular belief, she need not be a virgin. Male unicorns can't tell the difference and are willing to be seduced by any young, pretty maiden. Especially if she has a basketful of carrots and apples.

2. Wait in a secluded area of a forest with the maiden in view. You will need to hide yourself for hours, staying perfectly still without falling asleep. Do not to leave the maiden alone for any length of time with the unicorn. We wouldn't have a plague of centaurs if it wasn't for the old adage, "Unicorns have more fun."

3. Under no circumstance tell the maiden you intend to slay the

unicorn. Only say you plan to catch one. There were several incidents in the twelfth century of maidens warning the unicorn, outwitting the hunters, and riding off with unicorns. Centaurs with single golden horns growing from their heads were a result.

4. When a shortage of maidens occurs, do NOT dress up a knight in women's clothes and hope the unicorn shall fail to notice the difference. This has been attempted countless times in the past. The unicorn will maul the man as soon as it hears an unnaturally falsetto voice, notices a beard, or sees the knight relieving himself while standing up.

5. When attracting female unicorns, proceed with caution. It is said that the female of the species have a much keener sense of detecting virginity than the males of the species. If you happen to be a youth just entering manhood, it is best to avoid the forest until you have sewn some seed, lest you attract the unwanted advances of female unicorns. If you do find yourself in such a predicament, try distracting the unicorn with rainbows and glitter. Of course, this only works for young wizards who happen to keep a satchel of rainbows and glitter at their belt. The rest of you are screwed. Literally.

—This public service announcement was paid for by the Coalition Against Endangered Species (CAES), and Villains for Violence (VAV).

Author's Note:

I really like lists. Grocery lists. Stories told in the form of lists. Clickbait lists—to my detriment. At the time I was working on this piece, I was experimenting with the idea of telling a story in a list. I sold this story to Daily Science Fiction. Because lists are such a large part of my life, I thought it was an appropriate way to start the collection.

Speed Dating Books

I didn't know what to expect when I went into the bookstore. All I knew was that the experience would be magical.

A gravelly voice projected itself from a Stephen King novel, "Hey, lady. You want some literary thrills? Get between these sheets." The book on the table of best-sellers flipped to its climax, exposing the juiciest part of the story. I turned my gaze to the floor, not ready to see so much. Really, I didn't even know the book.

I backed away, past the shelves of dusty volumes in the used bookstore, scanning the spines for a good match. The tattooed, purple-haired bookstore clerk behind the register didn't look up from his sketch of a robot as I walked by. I hesitated at the display of romances. One of the books bounced up and down, unable to contain itself. "You know you want to take me home and rip off my dust jacket."

Even as I edged away, it continued to call after me. "I want to feel your bookmark between my pages."

Perhaps other readers were drawn to the forwardness of these books. I definitely wasn't. Passing the romance and mystery section, I pretended not to hear the books' cat-calls. I stopped at the next shelf, thinking I would be safe in the classics.

A hardback on a stand opened, fluttering its pages like eyelashes. A sultry, feminine voice said, "Who's afraid of Virginia Woolf? Not you. I bet you like to curl up with a good book at night."

I blushed, wishing I wasn't so transparent. No matter what my friends and family said, I would never find *Jane Eyre* or *Orlando* boring. More than anything, I wanted to lie in bed and leisurely peruse a novel. Of course, not just any novel would do. I wanted the right one for me.

I reached for *A Room of One's Own*, hesitating when the book continued on. "I'm a big book with big words. Are you woman enough to handle that?"

Other hardbacks called out to me. "Vonnegut laid tonight?"

"Wanna Faulkner?"

These were classics behaving like this? Books at the library never acted this way. I glanced around the nearly empty bookstore. An older man on the other side of the shelves stared through bifocals, practically drooling over two paperbacks on a shelf rubbing up against each other in a suggestive way.

I wandered from section to section, feeling more lost than ever.

Was literature in bookstores always so risqué? I had been a frequenter of the library up until I'd become too busy with my new job as a chemist to find time to read. My previous relationship with book loans had always left me feeling unsatisfied. Maybe it was knowing I had a finite amount of time to finish that book and I felt rushed. Or knowing those books were never truly mine and it was best not to grow too attached. Now that my work schedule had become less demanding and I had time to read again, I wanted something more than a temporary relationship with a novel. I wanted a keeper.

"Is this your first time in a bookstore?" someone asked from behind me. I whirled, toppling over a stack of paperbacks. I found myself face to face with the clerk. Centipede tattoos sprawled across his neck and peeked out from under the sleeve of his T-shirt, intermingling with inked spiders and scorpions. His purple Mohawk loomed over me.

"Um, well, it's been a while," I lied.

One side of his mouth quirked up into a lopsided smile, like he knew I'd never been in a bookstore. "Maybe you need a book that will take things a little slower? Speed dating books isn't for everyone."

"What do you mean? Speed dating?"

He waved a tattooed hand at the shelves. "People have less time and patience than they used to. They want everything *right now*. And they don't bother with the courtship of books. So novels have had to change to meet these demands. But, just like people, some books have a specific idea how things should be done. Particularly books with an older copyright date."

He gestured for me to follow him into a little side room. Faded volumes filled the shelves on the walls. The two plump couches and beaded lamps gave the room a cozy and inviting air.

The bookstore clerk eyed my grandmother's tweed coat over my work clothes and my Mary-Jane shoes. "My guess is you'll like these classics. They're less outspoken in here." Apparently reading the skepticism on my face, he added, "Trust me. I've been working as a book matchmaker for years."

He left me. It certainly was quieter.

I scanned a bookshelf, stopping at Jane Austen's section.

"Hello. I'm *Sense and Sensibility*. Nice to meet you," the maroon book in front of me said in a British accent.

"Oh, um, I read you already. It was from the library," I said, feeling awkward and embarrassed. I quickly added, "We were good friends. But it just didn't work out."

"Have you tried *Emma*? *Pride and Prejudice*? Maybe one of them will be what you're looking for."

I had heard a lot of good things about Jane Austen's other works. Especially *Pride and Prejudice*. At the library, two of the three copies had been "lost," or possibly stolen due to its popularity, and the one copy left had always been checked out. Considering I had fifty other unread books on my wish list, I figured I'd get to it eventually.

I selected a once-black book, the fabric cover now faded to gray.

A deep male voice cleared its throat. "Be gentle. I'm . . . a second edition." Something about the sheepish hesitation in the refined British accent caught my attention.

I smoothed my fingers over the faded embossing on the worn cover. The yellow pages were ragged and uneven. I opened to the title page. *Pride and Prejudice* by Jane Austen. If this was a second edition, this book had to be two hundred years old.

I carefully returned the novel to the shelf. "I wouldn't be able to afford you."

He chuckled, not in a superior and arrogant manner. It sounded as though he was tickled by the idea. "I would like to say I'm worth it, but that would come across as prideful and immodest, wouldn't it?

The truth is, I'm not as expensive as you'd think. I have some water damage. And my first owner dog-eared my pages."

I picked up the book again, noticing the way the thick paper crackled as I turned the pages. I rubbed a thumb over the fray of hand-stitched binding. In the pencil on the interior was the price: sixty-five dollars.

"Tell me a little more about yourself," I said. I glanced out the door of the side room. The little old man was now watching *Fifty Shades of Grey* whip sequels with bookmarks.

"Call me old fashioned," *Pride and Prejudice* said. "I'm a book that starts with character and setting before building up to the plot. I take things slow with my reader. I realize that isn't for everyone."

My heart skipped a beat. This classic sounded perfect. But I didn't want to rush into anything. Even with water damage, it was expensive.

"You don't have to make a commitment now. You can sit and get to know me before you decide if you want to take me home."

I sat on the couch, cradling the book in my lap as I read. I lost track of time, completely engrossed in the story.

The bookstore clerk cleared his throat from the doorway. "We're closing in ten minutes. Are you going to buy that or come back tomorrow and read some more?"

My pulse quickened when I considered how *Pride and Prejudice* might not be here if I waited until after work tomorrow. I smoothed my hand over the worn cover and gazed fondly at the novel.

"It is a truth universally acknowledged, that a single book in possession of a good plot must be in want of a reader," *Pride and Prejudice* said.

Without a doubt, I had found the right book for me.

Author's Note:

I love Mr. Darcy and *Pride and Prejudice*. He comes up quite a bit in my stories. Someday I will create a collection of stories with him as the central theme, but I need to write a few more first. This story first appeared in *New Myths*.

Debbie Does Delta Draconis III

I woke, sweaty and disheveled, aware I'd had that voyeuristic dream again: Worb, Dianna Tori, holodeck, no clothes . . . tangled in positions no man has done before. Why couldn't I have normal dreams about George Clooney like other middle-aged women? I dreamed about men from a science fiction television show with oversized craniums, wearing unfashionable bodysuits from the nineties.

When I walked into work, my long blonde hair clipped in place and my power suit speaking of professionalism, a flash of Dianna Tori draped in a Roman toga flashed before my eyes. I smiled, gazing off into the distance before catching myself.

Rita, our receptionist at Anderson & Sons, Attorneys at Law, stared at me, an eyebrow raised. "Good morning, Deborah," she said, a smirk twisting her lips upward. I trudged to my office, all the while feeling like a scarlet letter was etched into my forehead.

It had been like this for weeks, vivid Star Journey dreams a geek would have given his vintage Commander Spot action figure for. I was a respectable lawyer; I had no room in my life to entertain such fantasies. But at the morning meeting, as my boss droned on about profit like a greedy Alpha Centurian, the image of Worb popped into my head again. Tall, dark and masculine, both noble and honorable, loyal to his crew and the primary directive. Worb would have made a good lawyer.

I sighed. Maybe if I actually liked my job I wouldn't dream about aliens. This wasn't exactly the career of seeking out justice and fighting for the rights of humanity I'd envisioned for myself as a lawyer.

"Ahem, Earth to Deborah," Mr. Anderson, my boss, said. His bald head with his fake, carrot-tinted tan made him look all the more Alpha Centurian. "Do you have the settlement information from yesterday's meeting with the Yamada's or are you too busy daydreaming . . . about Captain Kurt?"

I snapped to attention, simultaneously confused and insulted. I would never like that womanizing, sexist Kurt. Why would he even suggest it? Sure, I had a "Kurt and Spot for president" business card in my wallet which I'd purchased online last election. . . .Had that weaselly Alpha Centurian been in my desk?

Everyone at the meeting laughed. My face burned with humiliation. I hated my job. I hated my life. No one understood me.

* * *

That night it was the same; Worb and Dianna Tori on the holodeck. Only this time, Worb looked at me. I was in the dream, too.

"I am not a merry man . . . yet." He held out his hand to me. "You want to join us. Come," he commanded in that deep, rumbling—and, um, slightly sexy voice. Okay, it wasn't slightly sexy, it was hot. I wanted him right then and there.

I became aware that Dianna Tori and Worb were standing in my room at the foot of my bed. The only thing that separated me from them was the fancy mosquito netting my ex-boyfriend had gotten me at World Market to make my room look exotic.

"I will recite poetry and you will throw furnishings at me," Worb said.

My heart gave a little flutter of joy. Considering this was foreplay for Denebians, that sounded appropriately Worb-like. I could do alien poetry. I drew the line when he waved his curved, semi-circular sword around in the air, slashing a bit of mosquito netting. I scooted back, my stomach flip-flopping with panic. He chanted in a guttural, alien dialect. The sharp blade flashed in the light, tearing a larger hole in the fabric. I ducked, too busy screaming in terror to pay much attention to the poetry.

Worb looked at Dianna. "Is screaming a customary reaction in the courtship between aliens and humans?"

She took something like a Kindle out from a pocket. "Are we going by Worb of Star Journey the Next Generator or Deep Nebula Three? Because there was that scene in DN3 when Dex and Worb—"

"I didn't watch Deep Nebula Three. I don't want a sword in my condo!" I screamed, almost hyperventilating. "I was a Next Generator girl."

I thought about throwing a pillow through the gaping wound in the mosquito netting, but decided a Denebian would probably like that.

Dianna hit him with the Kindle-like device. "Moron, you didn't do your homework. She didn't watch that scene."

"Oh, qu'vatlh guy'cha b'aka!" He sighed, looking downtrodden.

Dianna Tori nudged Worb out of the way. She gazed into my eyes. "This is all a dream. All just a dream. . . ."

My eyesight blurred and I slipped off into another dream. In this one, my boss's head was eaten by a giant squid.

In the morning, I noted the tear in my mosquito netting. My stomach quivered like a Tribolite after eating poisoned grain.

* * *

Like any sane person grounded in reality, I decided Worb could not be real. In addition to having erotic Star Journey dreams, I must have also been a sleepwalker and had slashed the mesh. To be safe, I put child safety locks on the kitchen drawers where I kept the knives.

I also took down the mosquito netting so I didn't have to be reminded of the dream.

It wasn't long before my next Worb dream. He was onboard some dark, dingy vessel in a sword fight with another Denebian. From the beginning, it was obvious Worb was going to win; the other guy was smaller, slower, and snarled like an Alpha Centurian. The opponent did have thick, lustrous hair, though that would hardly help him in a battle. A bunch of rowdy, armor-clad Denebian warriors shouted encouragement to them. I noticed the way sweat hung like jewels in Worb's mane of hair, the way he grunted in an oddly enticing way. He twirled in slow motion, tearing down his opponent and letting the other Denebian drop to the ground.

He turned to me, lifting his chin. "Do I please you now? Do you wish me to ravish you?"

The scene behind him faded and we were in my bedroom once

SARINA DORIE

again. Something wasn't right about this. For one thing, the guy on the floor was trying hard not to giggle.

I crossed my arms. "No, not really."

"See, I told you not to use the word 'ravish,'" the blood-covered Denebian on the floor said.

His voice sounded a bit like Dianna Tori's. Come to think of it, that gorgeous hair was like Dianna's too.

Worb slumped, looking uncharacteristically dejected. "I have traveled across the universe to seek you out and discover your passion for alien life, yet you spurn my advances?"

"You're saying you came to Earth for me?" It sounded like a line some college-aged guy would tell a girl. But I wasn't a naive freshman. I was a thirty-five-year-old lawyer. I didn't believe in true love. Nor did I believe fantasies could come true.

"What reason would I come to this barbaric planet other than for you and to fulfill your primitive desires?" Worb asked.

Hmm. Classic avoidance of answering the question. I turned to Dianna Tori/Denebian. "So why did you two really come here?"

He/she sat up, the sword falling aside. "To have encounters with lots of exotic alien females." Yes, that was definitely Dianna Tori's voice.

"No, that's not it! I only want you." Worb whispered through clenched teeth to his companion. "You aren't helping."

Typical immature male—some things were constants in the universe. "So you came to my planet to have sex with as many alien women as possible."

"And to film his sexual encounters," Dianna Denebian Tori added.

Worb looked like he was going to blow a warp core converter.

"You use unwitting women for your pornos? Then you sell them back on your alien planet?" I asked. This sounded like an interplanetary lawsuit waiting to happen.

"It's for interplanetary studies. It gets our tuition paid through the Intergalactic Yesselhynveeerka Academy," Worb said. "And we're not into the alien probe thing. That's just dirty."

College students, just as I thought. "And what do these women get out of it?"

"Ahem, their sexual fantasies are being fulfilled. I don't understand why you aren't behaving like the females portrayed in

10

television broadcasts when men satisfy their carnal desires."

My face flushed with anger. "There's a difference between fantasy and reality. It's one thing for a woman to daydream about having sex with a stranger. It's another for a stranger to force himself on her, claiming that's what she wanted. This is about consent. You're violating the people of my planet."

Dianna Denebian's face crumpled up in concern. "I can see this has upset you greatly. I had no idea this would cause humans to feel so ill-used. I apologize. How can we atone for this?"

I eyed her suspiciously, uncertain whether she was being sincere. There was something oddly rehearsed about her words. "You can start by erasing all recordings you've made of your sexual encounters."

Worb cast a dirty look at Dianna. "Well, that's an easy one, considering some Gloop Worm brain accidentally hit the erase button on all my previous alien exploits a month ago."

I raised my voice. "You also need to stop going into dreams and enacting fantasies without permission. And don't tell me you asked permission while in a dream state. The conscious mind is what counts in a court of law."

Dianna nodded emphatically.

Worb flashed the kind of smile that would have made any geek girl's heart flutter. Except mine, of course. "So, uh, now that we got that all out of the way, may I fulfill your fantasy?"

I threw the water bottle on my nightstand at him. It hit his crinkly forehead with a satisfying thunk.

He smiled. "Was that a yes?"

"Get out of my dream." If I was lucky, I would dream of a giant squid eating my boss and my clients. Now there was a fantasy I could look forward to.

* * *

The next day as I scanned my papers in the courtroom, I turned to my crack-smoking, child-neglecting, nightmare client to remind her to look like she felt remorse for dropping a TV on her ex-boyfriend's leg.—Ugh! I hated my job.—I was also about to ask her to stop flicking her lighter when I noticed a Denebian sitting a few rows back.

There were only a dozen people in the courtroom, so he was pretty noticeable. Worb smiled smugly. Did he think this was fulfilling some kind of fantasy? This was just plain annoying.

I nudged my client. "Could you do a small favor for me? Could you look over your shoulder and tell me if there's a man sitting about six rows back who looks a little, um, well . . . like a. . . ." I couldn't bring myself to say Denebian.

Her eyes went wide. "Oh my god! It's him!"

"You see him too, then?"

She started to hyperventilate, her voice rising. "Taylor, I love you!"

Judge Wentworth banged the gavel, looking irritated and grumpy. Nancy Yearborne, defending the drug-dealing, mini-mart robbing jerk who probably deserved to get a TV dropped on his leg, glanced over her shoulder, then turned her whole body to stare at Worb.

Nancy's face flushed. "Is that Taylor Lautner?" She unclipped her French twist and tossed back her head.

Is that who they saw?

The jurors whispered amongst themselves. I heard a few excited cries of, "Jacob!" and then, "No, it's Edward!"

The whispers rose into shrieks. Judge Wentworth continued banging his gavel. Suddenly he ceased. Putting on his glasses, he said, "That looks like Rock Hudson." From the gleam in his eyes, I guessed he had something of a crush on the late actor.

The courtroom was in sudden chaos, women jumping over the benches like hurdles, screaming the names of whoever they desired. Panic crossed Worb's face as he vanished in a Star Journey-like transporter beam.

This had to be a dream.

I pinched myself. Damn, I was definitely awake.

* * *

When Worb arrived that night, I was ready for him with a restraining order and papers for the lawsuit: Earth vs. Yesselhynveeerka, or whatever his planet was called.

Worb stomped his foot, his voice turning annoyingly whiny. He actually seemed to shrink in size. "I've been patiently waiting for the day you'd do some kinky Denebian n'ga'chug with me, playing this stupid alien in your dreams for a month, and this is the thanks I get?"

"Worb is not stupid!" I said.

He snorted in a very un-Denebian like way. "Do you really think aliens have crinkly foreheads? Ha! You wouldn't know what a hot, sexy alien looked like if . . . if he was in your room, like I am right now." He crossed his arms, looking especially sulky . . . and slightly greener, the edges of his body blurring. "Stupid human females! I'm trying to do a favor for you and you go off about primitive ethics. We should go to back to California. Those girls were begging for me as Justin Bieber. Or better yet, Edward."

Dianna looked up from the papers she was writing on. "I'm not playing Bella again. She lacks character development and is a poor female model with her needy dependence."

I turned to her. "Exactly! She's always relying on one of the male characters to rescue her. I really don't think she's a good example of the average human woman."

Worb growled.

"That's why I suggested a lawyer." Dianna's face brightened, a glimmer of green alien shining through the human skin. "I thought you would be a better representation of your culture. Someone intelligent and confident, someone who chooses a mate for more than superficial qualities. And there were other reasons I thought a lawyer who wants to make a difference in the world would be ideal. . . ."

My face flushed with warmth. I was flattered, but I kept my expressionless Commander Spot face on, not wanting these aliens to believe I could be manipulated.

Dianna circled something in the papers and handed them back to me. "There are a few misspellings. And Yesselhynveeerka is the academy, not the planet, but you're going to get a greater response from notifying the school anyway. It's just a lost cause to sue the government."

"Don't help her! I don't need this on my school records," Worb whined.

Dianna's tone was icy. "I told you a month ago, recording humans while procreating without their consent would be violating their culture."

Hmm. . . .Previously, Dianna had acted surprised when I'd been angered by the sexual dream invasion. And Worb had said she'd "accidentally" erased all his porno recordings . . . one month earlier. My heart raced with the realization that Dianna had planned on her lowlife-form boyfriend and school getting sued for something she hadn't agreed with. How sneaky, how cunning, how logically

Commander Spot-like. This was just like that one episode when Spot had to pretend to be a Xylanthian in order to help the oppressed people of that world. My respect for Dianna quadrupled.

Worb looked from me to Dianna. "Great. My girlfriend—" presumably ex-girlfriend, "—and the lawyer are getting it on while my school and I are getting sued. I'm done here." Worb walked through the wall.

Dianna rolled her eyes and held up a glowing blue cube in her hand. "Not without the keys." She turned to me. "I apologize for the inconvenience this has caused you." She sat down beside me, her human appearance crumbling further. Pulsing streams of green and dazzling lights flickered under her skin. "We don't copulate like your species does to procreate, so sexuality is novel for our people. My major is Earth studies and I came here on a scholarship to study your species. I've only recently begun to understand the complexities of your culture and how offensive and sexually demoralizing the idea of 'reality shaping' and 'dream bending' would be for humans. Once here, it was quite easy to find another Yesselhynveeerkan whose behavior toward humans I could document for my thesis on the violation of indigenous cultures."

I stared at the Dianna alien shimmering in and out of reality before me. One moment she was a ball of light shifting into the shape of a human, each tendril of hair coiling and bobbing like seaweed in an ocean's current. Another moment, she faded into a green Andromedan slave dancer, another Star Journey fetish I'd be embarrassed to admit. Then she flickered back into Dianna Tori. I forced myself to concentrate on her words, not all the alien fantasies she mirrored from my head.

"Will you stop shifting!" I said. "It's distracting."

"I'm not shifting, your subconscious desires are changing. Reading these brain waves comes naturally to my people. We energetically take on the environment and subconscious thoughts of sentient life forms around us. We're the equivalent of chameleons in the way we adapt to new surroundings." She flickered into a collage of donuts and bonbons, the aroma of rocky road and butter pecan wafting toward me.

I closed my eyes. My mouth watered. "What your race can do is the equivalent of a hologram fantasy. Humans might actually like the experience. Has anyone ever suggested telling humans about what you're doing instead of tricking them into it? If you plan to record them, you could offer them pay—though it's very possible they would be lining up to pay you to fulfill their fantasies. You could even sign a contract with them to prove you're doing something legitimate. You would need a lawyer for that, of course. . . ."

One of Dianna's floating strands of hair brushed against my shoulder. A ripple of pleasure shuddered through me.

"The people of my planet would benefit from hearing this proposal, in addition to being held accountable for the lawsuit you've drawn up. Would you be interested in traveling to Delta Draconis III and meeting real aliens?" She leaned closer. "I promise we aren't all like Glick."

A quiver rushed up my spine. Delta Draconis? Real aliens? Being abducted from my annoying clients to do something of intergalactic importance? Maybe fantasies did come true.

Author's Note:

Like so many of my stories, this title hints at a humorous, slightly risqué nature, though the content of the story is more silly and quirky than racy. Yes, I am a Star Trek fan. How much so? In my spare time I belly dance as an Orion, indentured-servant dancer for a theatre group that puts on Star Trek episodes in the park called Trek Theatre. And yes, I do dream about Star Trek. The inspiration for this story came after I dreamed about Worf and Deanna Troi. This story was originally published by *Perihelion Online Science Fiction Magazine*.

Eels for Heels

"Just doing my job. No need to thank me for rescuing you," Mervin said, salty spray splashing all around us. "Even if this is the third time, Kerstin."

Mervin was not the kind of merman that a girl throws herself off a cliff to be rescued by. He was potbellied, middle-aged and had thinning, blond hair.

Mervin held a firm arm around my waist as he swam through the less choppy waters toward the shore.

"What happened to that other merman, the handsome one with silver hair?" I shouted over the rush of waves. It would have been nice if he'd been the lifeguard on duty.

"It's his wife's birthday." Mervin's smile was smug.

"What about the one with blue hair?" Now he was a real catch.

"He only works on Monday, Wednesday and Friday. But anyway . . . you're not exactly his type."

"What does that mean? Are you saying I'm too human? Or is it my feet?" I have blonde hair and blue eyes just like my mermaid grandmother—though my hair color comes from a bottle. I lack the tail of a full-blooded mermaid, but I do have, well, eels for feet. Long story.

"It's not like that. Your feet are cute, honest." Mervin winced when one of my eels bit him. "It's just that Gordon . . . has a boyfriend."

Just my luck. "Are all the good mermen either gay or married?"

"No, some of us are divorced." He winked at me.

I ignored his last comment. "Aren't there any young, attractive mermen left on the California coast?"

He flashed a wicked smile. "Besides myself?"

I groaned. "You're not young." I didn't add attractive. After all, he had rescued me . . . again. I didn't want to be rude.

Mervin grimaced. "Well, considering it looks like you're pushing thirty yourself, I wouldn't be complaining."

I stiffened, another reminder of my impending doom. Almost thirty.

"Hey, you wanna come back to my place? My shift ends at seven and I have fish sticks you can nibble on."

"Pervert." I elbowed him and pushed him away.

My ruse over, I dove under the waves, contentedly breathing with my gills. The water was calmer closer in, and with a few strokes, the waves were shallow enough to walk in. It was there on the beach that I collapsed and cried. Almost thirty. I only had three months left to find my true love and get him to fall in love with me or my curse would last forever.

* * *

My problems all began with a pair of high heels back when I still had normal feet. It was the day after Thanksgiving, and there was a big shoe sale at Prada, just like everywhere else. The store was mobbed with humans and magical folk. I waited for six hours in the rain, endured my double mocha being jostled out of my hands and onto my cream sweater, and was pushed to the back of the lines several times by more aggressive customers. I was not in a mood to be trifled with.

When I finally squeezed into the store, I quickly became wedged between an elderly woman who smelled of apples and an immense woman I guessed to be a troll from the abundance of hair. I tried on a pair of size six-and-a-half red pumps that were just a pinch too small.

I was pretty desperate at this point as I needed something red and kitty-heeled for the STS Charity Auction (Save the Selkies) I was going to on Saturday night. I scavenged for a larger size among the multitude of shoes and reaching arms. Just as I was about to give up, a pair of size seven, red shoes shimmered in the pile, glowing with an unreal, magical quality. They slowly levitated toward me. I couldn't believe it. I snatched them up, put them on, and fell in love. Best of all, they were eighty percent off!

"Ahem," said a high, squeaky voice.

I turned around to see a tall, thin woman with green seaweed-like hair and a glittering sharkskin suit glowering at me. I scooted to the side, thinking maybe she wanted to get past me. I didn't mind. I had my shoes. She could be squashed between the old lady and the troll if she wanted.

"Ahem," she said again, eying those perfect red pumps on my feet. "Those are my shoes."

I smiled politely. "I'm sorry. You must be mistaken."

Her pale face turned a splotchy red. "I used a summoning spell for a size seven pair of red high heels and you took them as they were about to float to me."

That explained the levitating. But I wasn't about to give up these shoes. This was Black Friday at Prada. It was first come first serve.

I hugged the shoes to my chest. "There's probably another set of shoes in there that will fit you. These are mine." I realized after I said it how selfish it sounded.

"Give me those shoes now," she growled.

I stumbled backward into a lady with sunglasses. The lady's lips drew back over fangs. Blood-red eyes glared at me over the dark rims of her glasses.

Vampire, ick.

I squeezed through the shoppers, trying to escape with my find, but the lady in the sharkskin suit prowled after me.

Steam rose up from the woman, sea shells and barnacles forming on her face and hands. Her eyes turned black. A sea witch. Not a good sign.

"How dare you show such disrespect to an elder of your own people. I should curse you . . . turn your feet into eels, then you'll never be able to go shoe shopping again." She cackled, but then started to cough. She did smell like a smoker.

"No!" I screamed. "Anything but that! I love my shoes."

Her thin lips spread into a malicious smile as she removed a coral wand from her sleeve. "I see I'm actually doing you a favor. If you don't change your vain and shallow ways and find true love before you turn thirty, your feet will remain as eels forever."

Find my true love before thirty and change my vain and shallow ways? She had to be kidding. Just one of those would be difficult enough.

"Security!" I screamed, but my voice was lost in the mob of shoppers. A blinding, bluish light surged from her wand.

In the short term, at least I had a pair of shoes for the party on Saturday. And I did get complimented on them. . . .Too bad I hadn't been able to wear them.

* * *

I haven't had much luck with being less vain or finding true love. It's a little hard to attract a mate when you have two fifteen inch, wiggling eels for feet. And they make it impossible to drive. I can walk normally, but I have to take public transportation. Because my feet are a hazard, I'm forced to keep them in unfashionable plastic boxes filled with water most of the time.

Not that I didn't try to get rid of the eels. But surgery and magic both failed.

By the time I turned twenty-nine, I resorted to internet dating and jumping off cliffs trying to catch a merman. Ordinarily, I wouldn't even date a merman, but I wasn't exactly the catch of the day, as far as a human man was concerned.

* * *

It was dark by the time I made it home on the bus from my encounter with Mervin. I stepped out of the plastic boxes and into the two inches of water on the plastic floor of my house. My slovenly roommate, Shelly, was a blue-haired water siren and didn't mind living in a house with a shallow pool built into the entire premises. She sat on the plastic couch, one leg up on the vinyl seat, the other with toes wiggling in the water like worms. I kept my distance from her as I trudged past to my room in case my feet decided to nibble on her perfectly shaped, webbed toes.

In my room, I switched on the computer and checked my email. Three from my mother and twenty-six spam. Nothing from the new internet dating site I had posted on. I had tried to be upfront this time, as the last few guys I went on dates with had run screaming when they'd seen my feet. The worst part was I hadn't lied to them about it. While talking on the phone with Jonathan, I'd warned him I had a slight deformity in my feet. . . .I guess that was understatement. And Bill, I'd told him about the eels, but I guess he must have thought it was a joke.

I started to compose a new ad on another site.

Blonde, blue-eyed, twenty-nine, attractive. Likes: strolls on the beach, sushi, and shopping. Looking for a single, HWP, open-minded man who is also searching for his true love. Please, no smokers. BTW, I have eels for feet.

Crabs, that was over twenty-five words! I'd have to pay another thirty dollars.

* * *

The next day I had an email in my inbox:

Eels for feet? Sounds like a curse from a wicked sea witch. Those ill-bred hags are always doing nasty spells like that for unjust reasons. Tell me a little bit more about yourself. I'm six-one, a hundred and ninety pounds, and athletic. I enjoy basketball, Spanish food and swimming. My ideal date would be sailing on my yacht or curling up on the couch and watching a good movie like Pulp Fiction. I am often told by ladies that I'm attractive, but the truth is I'm just too busy to pursue dating as I'm the C.E.O of an international business and dealing with minor curses of my own. LOL! Email me if interested.

Sincerely,

M.J.

Eew, he thought Pulp Fiction was a good movie? But he did have a yacht and he was rich and potentially attractive. Was it shallow to consider him because of those reasons? On the other hand, he didn't mind the idea of eel feet, so if I dated him because of that, I would be less shallow. I was trying to work on both aspects of my curse, after all.

I waited a few hours to write him back—I didn't want to sound too eager. I told him a little more about myself, asked him to send a photo if he didn't think that would be too pretentious, and gave him my phone number.

When he emailed me back, he said he didn't have any good photos of himself, but asked to see one of me. He said he preferred to email, as that fit into his busy schedule better. Just the fact that he wanted to see a photo of me, but wouldn't send one of him (obviously that meant he was ugly), would have been a deal breaker right there, except for the fact that I had less than three months to find my true love, and he was the only man who had written. That, and I reminded myself I was trying not to be shallow. So that meant even if he was ugly, I shouldn't necessarily exclude him.

In the following days of email correspondence, I continued to frequent the beach in the evenings, as I did need a backup plan just in case M.J. didn't turn out to be the one for me. But I stopped throwing myself over cliffs, as I was starting to feel a little hope. Unfortunately, I still ran into Mervin while he was on the job. I did my best to ignore him and his corny jokes.

After two weeks of what seemed like endless emails, my deadline ticking closer, M.J. still hadn't asked me out on a date. I emailed him:

Here's the thing, I have just two months to break my curse. If I don't find my true love, I'm going to be cursed with eel feet forever. No pressure or anything. I realize this is the kind of thing that scares men off, but I'm not asking for a long term commitment, marriage or anything like that. I just need to find someone who can be my true love and break this curse.

He immediately emailed back and suggested a Spanish restaurant the following night.

I looked down at my feet. "Well, girls, it looks like we're going on a date."

* * *

I stomped as gracefully as possible into the crowded Spanish restaurant, my feet clunking in the water-filled plastic boxes. I ignored the stares. Those unfashionable blue boxes always drew unwanted attention.

The dark-eyed woman behind the desk greeted me and asked me a question. But my attention was on the man sitting alone in the middle of the restaurant. He wore a red, Hawaiian print shirt and he had feet—which I later realized meant he was, of course, a shape shifter. I focused on the blond, receding hairline even before he turned his head and I saw his face. Mervin. Or M.J. as he had recently called himself in his emails.

I felt a panic attack coming on. He was my prince charming? No, this wasn't fair. He had read my personal ad and had known it was me when I'd mentioned the eel feet. Not too many other girls have that problem.

Then anger flushed to my face. That dirty sea urchin! That's why he'd kept his name secret and hadn't sent me a photo of himself. If I wasn't in public, I would have unleashed the eels on him. I clomped over to his table.

Mervin's blue eyes widened at the sight of me. "Well, what do you know, it's the damsel in distress. How are the girls?" He glanced at my boxed feet.

So it had come to this. The only man who was remotely attracted to me was a middle-aged, overweight lifeguard who I doubted had a yacht.

"How dare you do this to me! I have feelings, you know. Tricking me into coming here just so you could—"

A slender blonde woman slid into the seat across from him, a polite smile on her pink lips. Her gaze darted to me, a question in her blue eyes. Mervin's brows were furrowed in confusion.

"Oh." I suddenly realized my mistake. He was on a date too, only his date was a beautiful woman half his age.

I hated this double standard. An unattractive, paunchy man could get a young, trophy girlfriend, but as soon as a woman got wrinkles or eel feet, she was destined to a life without love—or sex.

Doubly humiliated, I turned away, my feet clonk-clonking back to the door. The Mediterranean-looking waitress kept asking if everything was all right as she trailed behind me.

A tall man about six-one strode through the door, his eyebrows raised in expectation.

"Excuse me, are you Kerstin?" he asked, his deep voice almost as beautiful as his chiseled face. He had the hint of salt and pepper at the temples of his black hair and bluish-gray eyes framed by thick, black lashes.

I felt myself melt a little, my recent embarrassment forgotten.

He smiled, his white teeth straight and perfect. "I'm M.J. Clarkson. Sorry I'm late. I drove over here as soon as I finished with work. I wish I'd had time to change." He looked down at the designer suit hugging his definitely muscular build and grimaced.

"No, you're . . . you're perfect," I stammered. Too good to be true, really.

"Do you want to sit down?" he asked.

I glanced at Mervin and his anorexic-looking girlfriend. Maybe she wasn't that thin, she just looked malnourished next to him.

"Maybe we could go to a different restaurant. I'm not really in the mood for Spanish food," I said.

"Nonsense." M.J. grabbed my arm and tugged me down the aisle. "You have to try the black bean salad. And the calamari is exquisite. Though. . . ." His gaze swept over Mervin as the lifeguard bit into a large, deep-fried ring. "The calamari is quite fattening."

* * *

Over the following weeks, M.J. never questioned me about why I had been cursed, nor did he ever ask me about the eels. Not wanting to be vain and shallow and only talk about myself, I allowed him to talk about his favorite subject—him. He spoke about every aspect of his life, no matter how banal: his yacht collection; his long and tedious day dealing with a short Frenchman with halitosis; or how he had to fly to L.A. in order to get a proper pedicure.

One evening after work, dressed in a casual designer dress that had only cost three hundred dollars, I was taking my eels for a walk on the beach—they always behaved better after a swim in real salt water.

I picked up a candy bar wrapper someone had dropped on the beach, stuffing it into one of the boxes in disgust. Humans were always leaving their litter on the beach. A minute later, I leaned down to snatch up a shredded latex balloon.

"Missed a piece," a familiar voice said, an arm reaching out for a bit half buried in the sand.

I looked up into Mervin's twinkling green eyes. He was out of breath, like he'd been running to catch up with me. "Haven't seen much of you lately. Glad to see you've given up jumping from cliffs. It's a dangerous hobby."

I nodded and continued walking, shifting the blue plastic boxes I used for shoes to my other arm. My blonde hair whipped around my face in the wind, hiding at least a little of the humiliation in my countenance from the misunderstanding at the Spanish restaurant.

"What's new with you?" he asked, a cheery smile on his face.

I shrugged. I didn't want to be outright rude, but I didn't want to encourage conversation either.

"So . . . do I, ahem, look any different?" he asked.

I glanced at the paunchy belly hanging over his Bermuda shorts that he was trying to suck in.

"I lost five pounds," he went on. "I'm on a seafood diet."

I rolled my eyes, smiling in spite of myself. "Is that a lame attempt at a joke? You eat everything you see?"

He laughed. "No, I just started Kelp Watchers. It's a diet plan for mer-folk. It involves a lot of raw fish and seaweed. No more fried fish and chips for me." He patted his belly.

"Mervin, you'll have to excuse me. I have a date tonight," I said, picking up speed, which I hoped would leave him in my dust—or sand, rather.

"Yeah? With M.J. Clarkson? He owns the biggest yacht manufacturing business in America."

"Actually, in the world," I corrected. M.J. had bragged about it in three emails and on two dates.

"Hmph. My daughter was placed as an intern at his company last year in college, but . . . I told her I thought there were other companies that would be better to work at. I don't like the way he treats his employees." Mervin's lips thinned, making him look even more goofy.

"Your daughter?" I asked. It never occurred to me that this man would have children.

"Yeah, you saw her the other night at Spanglish. She gets her good looks from her mom, not me."

My cheeks grew hot just at the mention of the Spanish restaurant.

Mervin continued on, "Sara's a business major and she was placed at the local branch of Clarkson Inc., but I didn't want her to work there, what with M.J. Clarkson's reputation and all."

I halted. "Reputation?"

"Yeah, he chases his secretaries around the desk. Or at least he used to."

I said through clenched teeth, "My boyfriend isn't a womanizer." If he had been, we'd have slept together by this point. But he'd said he wanted to be sure I loved him first. Incredibly romantic, right? That, and the eels had gotten out of their boxes while we were making out and bitten him.

"Maybe not, but there's something fishy about him. He's a rich guy whose M.O. is chasing after women. He doesn't seem like the kind of guy who would date someone with a curse. I think he's using you."

"Has it ever occurred you that I'm using him?"

Mervin's eyes were round and regretful. "If that's the case, I'm afraid that isn't going to help you find true love either."

* * *

The poison of doubt began to nag at my mind. What if I was just using M.J. to break my curse? Did that make me . . . vain and shallow? Not that finding my true love before thirty in itself was such a bad idea, but maybe I was going about this the wrong way.

I asked M.J. that night while he was driving me home from our date, "I'm worried about my curse. I only have fifteen days left to break it and my feet are still eels. Do you love me?"

M.J. wrapped an arm around my shoulders and kissed me when the traffic light turned red. "Curses aren't cured in one night, pumpkin."

I glanced at his perfect hands and feet. Like he knew anything about curses.

He smiled, oblivious to my melancholy. "I should take you on my jet this weekend and we'll fly into Seattle and go shopping. Wouldn't that be fun?"

I nodded, but for once shopping didn't appeal to me. In fact, I cancelled on Friday night and told him I had the flu, which was a lie. I just didn't think shopping was what I needed.

I had this romanticized image that once I met my true love, my curse would—poof—disappear. But maybe M.J. was right. Curses didn't disappear in one night. Love at first sight was for movies. Besides, I still had to work on not being shallow.

"How does one really become unshallow?" I asked Shelly as she sat watching some reality TV show about an interracial vampire-werewolf marriage. If anyone would know how to not be vain, it might be a sea sprite with blue hair who wore threadbare sweats.

"You could start by not wearing designer clothes all the time. Oh, I know! You could talk to people you would consider to be socially beneath you."

I forced myself to look at images of ugly people on Facebook and tried to find good things to say about them—while wearing sweats I borrowed from Shelly's closet. I figured that was a good warm up.

Shelly splashed through the water and eyed my outfit from the doorway. "Now if you really want to prove how unshallow you are, you should wear my clothes outside the house on a date with your boyfriend."

A squeak of noise escaped my lips. There was no way I was going to wear these sweats outside of the house, especially not in the presence of M.J.

I tried to think of an excuse that wouldn't make me . . . vain. "He's out of town."

She shrugged. "You could wait until he comes back. Or you could go out with . . . Mervin."

"I can't cheat on my boyfriend!"

"You can still go out with friends, can't you?"

So it was that I offered to buy Shelly dinner, if she went down to the beach with me to see if Mervin would come with us. Considering how curt I'd been to him the last time I'd seen him, I was surprised he was willing to even talk with me. Then again, when Shelly shouted, "And Kerstin's buying!" who would object?

We waited another half hour until Mervin got off work and then for his tail to dry and change back into legs so he could drive. Wouldn't it be nice if I could do that with my feet?

Shelly said over the roar of the engine from the back seat, "I hear there's a great new Spanish restaurant."

I gagged at the thought of more Spanish food. Almost every date I'd had with M.J. had been at Spanish restaurants.

"Since I'm buying, I get to decide where we eat. Mervin is on a seafood diet and I want sushi, so we're going to Miso Happy."

As we ate dinner, it was refreshing not talking about Armani suits, yachts, or how ugly and annoying all the people who worked for M.J. were.

Mervin unlatched my plastic eel boxes and fed them bits of fish during dinner. It was kind of nice. I almost forgot I had sweats on.

Then Shelly blurted out, "Kerstin has a curse. That's why she has eel feet and has to find her true love before her thirtieth birthday this month."

My face burned with embarrassment. It wasn't like Mervin didn't know about the curse, but I'd never mentioned I was almost thirty.

"Oh? So you won't get over-the-hill cards on your thirtieth, you'll get over-the-eel cards?"

So not funny.

Shelly opened her mouth again, about to make me die even more inside, but Mervin patted his belly and changed the subject. "Well, this was an excellent dinner. And I didn't go off my diet. I've lost twelve pounds in the last month."

Shelly nodded, blue hair bouncing. "That's pretty good."

I wasn't sure what to say that would sound conversational. I tried my best. "Well, it's good you're trying to be healthy. You might not die of a heart attack that way."

Shelly made a face at me. Yeah, after I said it, I realized it was a shallow thing to say. But nothing I ever said fazed Mervin. Which is why I was so shocked to see tears in his eyes.

He laughed, trying to make a joke out of it like he did with everything. "Better to be a washed up buoy than a washed up Bowie. Heh." He was silent a moment, before adding. "My brother just died of a heart attack about six months ago."

"I'm sorry," Shelly said, kicking me under the table.

"Yeah. I'm sorry, too," I added.

"He was only forty-four—three years older than me. It was a wake-up call, really. I decided to eat healthier, cut down on the beer, and switched to a less sedentary job." His optimistic smile was forced. "And believe me, rescuing beautiful women from drowning as a lifeguard is far more exciting than being an accountant ever was."

I gazed at Mervin, really seeing at him for the first time. His eyes were a vivid green and when he smiled, you couldn't help smiling along with him. He wasn't ugly, really, he just wasn't . . . perfect like M.J. Mervin had his problems, too, like everyone else. I'd just never considered what anyone else's might be.

I'd never considered anyone else. Period.

And then it dawned on me. I wasn't cursed with eel feet because I hadn't found my true love, I was still cursed because I was a selfish bitch, too shallow to care about other people.

* * *

Mervin invited Shelly and me to his seafood barbeque. When I told M.J. about it, he grumbled and then grumbled some more when I actually made him go. Because I didn't wear an expensive cocktail dress and instead wore a summery, vintage dress, he complained again. In my attempt to be less self-absorbed, I made an effort to ask the people I met questions to prove I didn't need to only talk about myself. "So, what do you do for a living?" I tried, or "How many kids do you have?" and "Where did you get those cute sandals?" Okay, I'll admit the last question was delving into dangerous territory, but I couldn't help myself.

"Would you stop doing that?" Sipping the chardonnay he'd brought to the barbeque, M.J. rolled his eyes. "I hate listening to conversations about people's mediocre lives."

I lifted my chin. "I dare you to try it. I bet you can't think of something you could ask someone."

It took him ten minutes, but he did it. "So, how do you know Kerstin?" M.J. asked Mervin.

"Oh, I rescued her from drowning a few times, returned her glass slipper to her when she left it at the ball, the usual," Mervin said with a wink.

I couldn't help laughing. Mervin could be pretty funny.

* * *

The days passed too quickly. I spent my extra time volunteering at a shelter for injured sea mammals, reading to the blind (and helping them pick out color coordinated clothes), and doing litter patrol on the beach with Mervin.

By the time it had whittled down to three more days to break my curse, I was in a constant state of panic. I took time off work, tried to meditate, and made out with M.J. in a vain attempt (actually it was a very, very unvain attempt) to induce true love, but I still had eel feet.

On the night before my thirtieth birthday, we sat on M.J.'s suede couch, watching Pulp Fiction in his penthouse condo. Unable to focus on the movie, I asked him half-joking, half-serious, "If I still have eel feet tomorrow, are you going to dump me?"

He laughed. "Of course not. We haven't broken my curse yet. After that, if you want to break up. . . ."

I glanced at his perfect hands and feet, uncertain I had heard him correctly. "Your curse? What curse?" Considering he'd told me about every other detail of his life, it was hard to believe I hadn't heard this before. I thought back to what Mervin had told me about something being off about M.J.

I hated the idea that he had been right.

He fidgeted with his collar. "Um, well, I have a curse too."

I crossed my arms. "And you failed to mention this because. . . ?"

He walked across the room to the bar and poured himself a whisky. "It's humiliating."

"God! You are so selfish sometimes. I bet that's what you were cursed for."

His face turned red. He gulped his drink.

"Well, was it? Or was it for chasing secretaries around the office?"

He poured himself another. "You wouldn't understand."

"You're right, because you've never told me."

He stared out over his balcony at the rolling waves of water. "I met her at a bar. I didn't realize she was a sea witch when I hit on her. She probably wouldn't have cursed me if I hadn't slapped her on the rump, but it wasn't my fault. I was drunk. . . .She gave me a, um, snake appendage and told me I wasn't going to be able get rid of it

28

unless I found my true love before my fortieth birthday—and thought of other people before myself." He certainly hadn't done very well with the latter.

This was my boyfriend? And I liked him . . . why? My gaze shifted to his handsome face.

I burst into tears. I wasn't any better than M.J. Well, maybe slightly better, but I was still just as vain as I'd always been.

"But I've changed," M.J. said. "I always ask women if they're sea witches before I hit on them. And I'm a much better listener than I used to be."

Wow, then he must have been a complete loser before.

"And I care about your curse, too. I mean, you would be more attractive without eels attached to your feet, and it would be easier if they didn't try to bite me when I get close to you, but don't forget, I want my curse gone, too." He gave a nervous laugh. "And once you're one hundred percent in love with me, you'll be able to help me with my curse. You'll love me for who I am and at last I'll return to my normal self and will be able to have sex with a woman again."

I glanced at the bulge in his pants and leapt away from him, at last understanding which appendage had been cursed.

Eew! Double eew! And I thought eel feet were bad.

* * *

It was a little after nine p.m. when I stomped into my home, the eels writhing in complaint. Shelly wasn't there. Not exactly unexpected as she didn't work Thursdays and tended to stay out until the bars closed on Wednesday nights. But I had kind of hoped she'd be home so I would have someone to talk to.

I didn't have any other friends. The normal ones had shunned me when my eel feet bit their carpets and I showed up everywhere without fashionable shoes. Unsure who else I could talk to, I walked the two miles to Mervin's apartment. I rang the doorbell about eight times before he answered.

He rubbed his groggy eyes, yawning. "It's the middle of the night, Kerstin. What's up? Either you have a craving for my delicious cooking or my delicious body."

I broke into tears for the second time that night. "I'm turning thirty in an hour and I'm alone, and I just want to be near another person who isn't afraid of my feet."

"Well, no one should have to be alone on her thirtieth birthday." He put an arm around me and let me in.

I sat on his couch as he made us hot cocoa with skim milk, and he let me tell him about my curse—and cursed day.

He unlatched one of the boxes that held my foot and stroked the eel. "So you have eel feet. Yeah, people don't consider them the sexiest feature in the world. But you know what? We've all got our faults. And eels aren't the worst thing in the world."

I glanced at his pajama pants. "You don't have any eels or snakes hidden under there, do you?"

"No." He laughed, probably thinking I was joking. "Really, Kerstin, your feet aren't so bad. You can still walk. And if someone really loves you, they aren't going to care about little things like that."

I covered my face with my arm, tuning out his attempt to be nice. "It's all people see when they look at me—the freak woman with eel feet."

He pulled my arm down so he could look me in the eyes. "That's not all I see when I look at you. You're a person who can admit your imperfections—and you're trying to fix them. Most people would give up if they were cursed like you, but you're tenacious. I admire that. Also . . . you look pretty hot in a bikini." He winked at me.

He unlatched the other box and stroked the eel within it. I sniffled again and he handed me a tissue. Then he went back to massaging the eels. It had been a long time since a man had looked at, let alone touched my feet.

I leaned back, staring at the ticking clock. Ten more minutes before midnight.

Mervin wrapped an arm around me, his gaze following mine. "I'm probably not your 'true love,' whatever that really means, but I do like you and care about you and want you to be happy. Even if your feet stay exactly the same, I don't mind. They're cute. And . . . I would like you to let me take you out on a date." Then he kissed me, the kind of kiss that made the world melt away and left me breathless. It was a kiss I would never have known if that sea witch hadn't cursed me.

And I thought, well, even if my eels didn't go away, at least Mervin genuinely liked me for who I was. And my feet probably wouldn't bite him if we tried to have sex. What more could a mermaid ask for?

Author's Note:

I love fairy tales and for me this was a modern fairy tale with a slightly different take on *The Little Mermaid*. One of the things I always hated about that story was how sad it was and how the mermaid has to give up her own happiness for the man's because it was written in an era when this was the expectation for a woman. I wanted my retelling to be fun and funny and be more about today's morals than those of the past. Like many of my stories, my main goal was to laugh and enjoy the journey writing for this. On a coincidental note, I wrote this when I was twenty-nine. The story originally appeared in *Roar Volume 5*.

The Quantum Mechanic

Marian's flashlight headband shone on the surface of the vacuum chamber she had slid herself into. She replaced the panel over the inter-cooling system of the cold fusion reactor she was servicing—or what her boss hoped would be a cold fusion reactor if it didn't explode this time—while she pretended she didn't hear him arguing with her sister again.

Dr. Malachlor's raspy voice was loud enough to hear from across the room and inside the machine. "There are highly sensitive experiments in this laboratory. Don't touch my equipment again."

Vana laughed. "Or what? You're going to spank me?" Vana could have read the ingredients on a cereal box and made it sound sexy. The sultrier her voice and the more flippant the comment, the more Marian could tell her sister's feelings were hurt.

There was a time she had envied the way Vana attracted the attention of any man she wanted—Marian's boyfriends included. Now after seeing her sister with two ex-husbands and currently in another unhappy relationship, she wondered if it had been a blessing being born the brainy brunette instead of the buxom blonde. At times like this, she told herself she was the lucky one. The times she ate dinner alone in her apartment reading blueprints, and cuddled up to manuals in bed, she didn't feel so sure. If only Marian hadn't confided in Vana how brilliant and handsome her employer was when Dr. Malachlor had first hired her, Marian might have had a chance to show him how sexy brainy brunettes could be.

Marian slid deeper inside the machine. She tilted her head so that the beam from the light attached to her headband shone on the next panel. Nothing was wrong with this section of the inter-cooling system, but it was slightly quieter here in the womb of the machine.

"Don't set that there!" Dr. Malachlor's muffled voice said. "That laser will split the atoms in your body apart and render you into a pile of incomplete particles."

"Ooooo, talk dirty to me, you big, bad atom-smasher."

"No! That's the cold fusion reactor." Marian could practically hear him tearing out his gray hair.

Vana tsked. "Viktor, you asked me to stop by your 'secret laboratory' to bring you lunch. The least you could do—"

"I swear, you do these things just to—Aaagh!"

The entire wall vibrated and a high-pitched screech buzzed in Marian's ears. She didn't know what they were doing out there, but it sounded like they had turned the reactor on.

With her inside.

Marian frantically pushed off from the wall ahead of her and squirmed back toward the open panel she'd climbed in. "Hey! I'm still in here. Turn the machine off," she shouted over the dull rumble.

Dr. Malachlor's voice rose above the thudding clunks of the machine, but she couldn't make out the words. The metal of the panels around her were warm to the touch. A brilliant white light blinded her. Marian squeezed her eyes closed and prayed she wasn't going to be rendered into a pile of incomplete particles.

* * *

Marian's head swam, the room spinning in a blur. She could barely breathe. Putting a hand to her ribs, she realized that constraining sensation was actually a corset under her dress. She blinked and refocused her vision on the screwdriver in her hand. Why was she holding a screwdriver? And why was she wearing goggles on her head instead of her flashlight headband?

Marian turned her head over her shoulder, studying the steam fusion generator that filled half the laboratory. The twisted jumble of wires disappearing into the heat chamber and the mass of tubes and valves connecting the steam exchange systems looked off. Instead of buttons there were levers and knobs. The screens were blank and there were gears. It didn't look like Dr. Malachlor had even turned it on today.

Although there was a familiarity to this machine, it also possessed a certain foreignness she couldn't put her finger on. Why did everything feel off?

She noticed the sticky heap of apples and pie crust spilled over the controls. From the plastic wrapped sandwiches and the unopened bottle of soda on the floor, she had a suspicion this might be one of Vana's accidents.

Dr. Malachlor sat at his computer, silver spectacles on his hawk nose as he squinted at the punches he made to his Babbage cards. Oddly, steam rose from the top of the computer.

"Where's my sister?" Marian asked.

Dr. Malachlor didn't bother to look up. "What sister?"

She rolled her eyes. She replaced the screwdriver in her toolbox and ducked under an arm of the generator to get the paper towels from the corner by the sink. Her bustle bumped against the machine.

The gas lights flickered and the sound of a pop and breaking glass came from the other side of the wall. Three confident knocks rapped at the door. Without waiting for an answer, a man peeked his head inside. Though salt-and-pepper speckled his temples and crow's feet crinkled the corners of his eyes, he would have deserved the "Mr. Eye Candy" label Marian's sister bestowed on good-looking men.

The man's gaze was glued to a flat device with knobs he held in his hand. "That should take care of that." He twisted one of the buttons and then tucked the screen into a pocket of denim overalls not so different from Marian's own. Well, not like Marian's own but what she imagined her fitted bodice should look like. He patted his pocket. "I'm here to fix a space-time continuum for a Dr. Viktor Malachlor."

Marian glanced at the open tool box he carried, filled with screwdrivers and wrenches as well as some futuristic-looking devices. His name tag read, "Bob." She reached for paper towels but instead found a pile of folded rags. Having no other options, she grabbed one and squeezed around the machine to clean up the spill.

"I didn't call a mechanic. Or a physicist," Dr. Malachlor said.

"No, the you in this dimension didn't. But another you did. Your experiments are interfering with another dimension's time." Bob checked off something on his clipboard and shoved it into the side of his tool box before stepping past Dr. Malachlor.

A quantum mechanic? Marian glanced at the steam fusion

machine. Could it be that it wasn't her? Reality was malfunctioning? Pi was still 3.2, right?

"Oh, no you don't. This is a secret laboratory." Her employer stretched out his arms to block Bob from going further, but the man stepped forward anyway, pushing Dr. Malachlor back.

Marian sighed. If Dr. Malachlor had paid for one of the more state-of-the-art, underground secret laboratories—or at least hired a receptionist to guard the entrance—it was far more likely his laboratory and experiments would have stayed a secret.

The stranger halted at the sight of Marian wiping chunks of apple from the controls. "Marian?" he asked.

The intensity of his gaze unsettled her. Something about his earnest face was familiar. He reminded her of that cute guy she sometimes saw eating at the hot dog stand down the street. Although, she was fairly certain that man was younger and had longer hair.

She glanced at Dr. Malachlor who had rushed back to his computer to turn off his screen. "Do I know you?" she asked.

"Not yet. But you will." He dropped his box of tools and swept her into his arms. He kissed her with such tenderness Marian suspected she wanted to know him in the future.

Still, it was the present that was important.

She pushed him back. "Excuse me, Bob. I don't know what you think—"

His blue eyes turned mournful. "I'm sorry, Marian. I haven't been able to do that since, well . . . the you in my time had a heart condition and we didn't know it. . . ." Tears filled his eyes. He cleared his throat and stepped back, though he held her hand in his, smoothing his thumb over her knuckles.

A buzz to her left caught Marian's attention. Dr. Malachlor stepped forward. "Get out of my laboratory. I've got steam power and I know how to use it." He held up what looked like a tuning fork attached to wires that connected to a pressure cooker. That was odd. Marian didn't remember a steam laser being in the lab.

Bob shook his head and tsked. "Wow, things really must be messed up. This world has our steam power and my world probably has your electricity."

Dr. Malachlor lunged forward, his quaint laser in hand. He didn't get very far with all the tubes connecting it to its power source. He was abruptly jerked backward and stumbled into his desk.

Bob turned to her again. "This world has our steam power and my world probably has your electricity. Wow, things really must be messed up."

Marian opened her mouth, about to say he had already said that. And it didn't make any more sense the second time around. To her further confusion, she noticed Dr. Malachlor slowly slinking backward.

"I've got steam power and I know how to use it. Get out of my laboratory," he said again.

Bob stepped forward. He smoothed his thumb over the back of her hand. The irritation in his blue eyes softened into sorrow. He stammered out an apology—the same apology he had just uttered before. Tears filled his eyes.

Her hand dropped from his chest and for a moment, she melted into his embrace as he kissed her. Her heart skipped a beat and she couldn't help noticing this kiss was better than the first one. She considered all the times she had stayed late at work instead of going out on dates, not wanting to be like her sister.

Still, it was the present that was important. This wasn't the present anymore, she realized. This had already happened moments ago. Everything was happening backwards.

Words spilled from her lips, her mind divided by what she now saw and what she had been thinking moments ago. "I don't know what you think— Excuse me, Bob."

Bob reversed his steps toward the door. "But you will. Not yet." The toolbox on the floor lifted into his hand.

Her lips moved and her voice came out despite her attempt to control it. "Do I know you?"

Marian tried to break out of the cycle, to say out loud what she now realized was happening, but her mouth wouldn't work. She tried to move her body in a new pattern, but instead she turned back toward the machine and pushed pieces of apple across the controls.

She listened to Dr. Malachlor's and Bob's repeated exchange of words as her boss now pushed the stranger toward the door. Marian shook with effort, trying to free herself from the backward pattern. It took great concentration to keep her thoughts from returning to what they had been the first time this had happened.

"I'm here to fix a space-time continuum for a Dr. Viktor

Malachlor." Bob twisted one of the buttons and then tucked the tool into a pocket of his denim overalls. "That should take care of that."

Marian lurched forward, falling to her knees—which were fortunately cushioned by layers of ruffles and petticoats. She was free. Bob placed a hand under her elbow, helping her to her feet. She exchanged startled glances with Dr. Malachlor. Like it or not, something was wrong with the space-time continuum. And they needed a quantum mechanic to fix it.

* * *

Dr. Malachlor pulled on his rubber gloves and paced the room. The quantum mechanic unscrewed a panel on the side of the steam-powered generator and stuck his head inside. Marian sat on the floor next to him, no easy task in a corset. She watched in fascination as he took apart the gears under the control board and rewired it. Whatever he was doing, she wanted to remember it. Time travel was far more interesting—and probably more lucrative—than failing at steam fusion again.

"So we actually made a time machine but hadn't realized it?" Marian asked.

"More like a time distortion machine. You've probably noticed things are a little off. That's because they don't belong in this space or time."

Marian glanced at the steam-powered laser next to the sink. "So you're from the future and a different dimension?"

"Yeah. Can you hand me that pair of pliers? Thanks."

Marian studied the spilled apple pie and the sandwich still on the floor. There was something about that, but her brain grew fuzzy and it became harder to remember what it was as the moments passed. Apple pie . . . a fight . . . who had spilled it? "Someone's missing from this time?" she asked.

"Yes, your sister, Vana. She's in a different dimension right now. The space-time continuum where I come from. That's why I'm here, actually. You think Dr. Malachlor has a hard enough time dealing with one Vana, imagine how hard it is on him with two of them." He laughed, the merry tone so contagious Marian joined in with him. He squeezed her hand, the gesture familiar and alien at the same time. "Can you hand me the molecular energy converter?"

Marian reached for one of the strange looking devices—a little clock with wires and suction cups attached to the ends. Then she saw another unusual tool with blinking lights and reached for that instead. She hovered between the two, then selected the suction cup clock. He didn't complain when she handed it to him, so she assumed she must have chosen correctly.

Bob closed the panel and screwed it back on. "Looks like my work here is mostly done." He sat up but made no attempt to move. His gaze lingered on her, causing her stomach to lurch. She'd never believed in silly things like love at first sight like—Who was it that believed in that? Oh yes, probably her sister. But the longer she spent with this man from the future, the more her heart yearned for someone to love her in the present.

Bob brought her fingers to his lips and kissed her knuckles. "You have no idea how much I've missed you."

As much as she pined to hear such words from a man, it was hard to believe. "But if you loved me, why haven't you gone back in time to prevent my death?"

He cupped her chin in his hands, his lips so close he could have kissed her. Instead he spoke softly. "Do you know how many dimensions there are? Every choice, every changed action at the last second splits and creates another reality. I've probably visited a hundred different dimensions by now and warned you. But I can't go back and change my time." He enveloped her in an embrace, tucking her head under his chin as they sat side by side. He smelled of brass and WD-40, everyday scents that she knew she was going to now associate with him.

He twined his fingers through her hair and kissed her forehead. Marian wished they could have stayed like that forever.

"Ahem. Are you done tampering with my steam fusion generator?" Dr. Malachlor demanded.

Bob rubbed at a pink scar along his jaw. "Yep." He pulled out his clipboard and rose, handing it to the doctor. "Just sign here and here and date over here."

Dr. Malachlor flipped through the pages, signing on the lines. He hesitated, reading over what he was signing.

Bob grabbed the clipboard and shoved it into his toolbox. "No need to read the fine print. It just says all people will return to their proper space-time zones, including, but not limited to people you might not want to see."

"Wait a minute. What does that mean? Who wouldn't I want to see?" Dr. Malachlor asked.

Bob winked at Marian and strode out the door.

Her heart lurched in her chest. She'd finally met someone—a man who was brilliant and handsome and was in love with her, brainy brunette tendencies and all—and he was leaving for a future where she no longer existed. And she would be alone again. She ran out after him. "Wait! Bob, I need to ask you something."

"Actually, you prefer to call me Bobby."

"Um, okay, Bobby. How do I—I mean, when will I meet you?"

"You've already informally met me a few times at the hotdog stand. And you'll meet me again very soon." He glanced at his watch. "Probably in about fifteen minutes."

She laughed. "You're from the future, so aren't you supposed to keep things like that a secret? You know, so the space-time continuum doesn't get messed up?"

He shrugged. "That rule book hasn't been invented yet. Oh, by the way, after I leave, you're going to need to excuse yourself from the room to evacuate the building so you won't get caught in the cross-fire of any exploding bolts or anything when the cold fusion generator blows." He pointed toward the window of the laboratory. A slate gray building could be seen across the street. Within, a figure sat at a desk. "And if you would be so kind to run to the building over there and save my life, I would be grateful. That's actually how you and I meet. And not that I'm one to complain, but you always say you wished you had taken the time to brush your hair before meeting me."

"What?" Marian glanced back through the open door. Dr. Malachlor was turning the machine on.

Bob squeezed her elbow.

"So to summarize: go to the ladies room to get Vana—that's where she should be now—brush your hair, evacuate the building, and then go over to my building on the third floor and save your future husband from dying in an inferno of fire."

"Got it," she said.

"Oh, and if you can remember any of this as time begins to correct itself, you may want to get your heart checked." He squeezed her to him and kissed her one last time. "And one more thing, on our first date when I ask you if you want to see my Tesla coil, that isn't an innuendo for sex." He handed her a list. "Don't lose this. It's to remind you of everything you need to do when you get back to your space-time."

She shoved it down into the safely of her corset, not wanting to lose it.

* * *

Marian blinked against the harsh white light. The reactor hummed all around her. She was inside the machine. She continued squirming out, surprised how easy it was to move as she wasn't wearing a corset. Dr. Malachlor stood in front of the reactor muttering to himself as he attempted to clean pie from the controls.

She shook his shoulder. "We have got to get out of here. The machine is going to explode."

Dr. Malachlor held up a gooey handful of apples. "Where is that sister of yours? She made a mess with pie all over the controls."

"Did you hear me? The quantum mechanic said your machine is about to explode!"

"He sabotaged my machine? I knew I shouldn't have signed those papers." He wiped his sticky hands on his lab coat and turned toward his computer.

Marian raced into the hall and pulled the fire alarm, the loud chime blaring all over the building. It wasn't likely many people were in the building, it being a Sunday morning, but she would take no chances.

Now what was she supposed to do? Her brain felt foggy. Oh, her sister! She raced down the hall to the public restroom. She found Vana applying lipstick. Her eyes were red and swollen.

"You wouldn't believe what that jerk just said to me in a future space-time," Vana complained.

"We need to evacuate. The cold fusion machine is going to blow."

Vana rolled her eyes. "Again?"

Marian glanced at the mirror. Her brown hair looked like a puff ball, sticking out with static around her flashlight-headband. She tore it off. "Hey, do you have a hair brush?" She'd left hers in her purse which was still in the lab. She wouldn't have time to retrieve it if the machine was going to explode soon.

Vana rummaged through her immense Coach purse. Marian grew impatient. She grabbed her sister by the elbow and dragged her toward the stairs. She hoped Dr. Malachlor was already out. Vana continued to look for a brush as they descended. Once out the front door, Marian left her sister on the sidewalk.

"Hey, I found the hairbrush!" Vana shouted after her.

"No time now," she called over her shoulder as she crossed the street to where Bob worked. "Call Dr. Malachlor on his cell phone to make sure he's on his way."

"Where are you going?" Vana asked.

"I need to go save my future husband."

Vana raised an eyebrow, her posture changing from frazzled to sex-goddess in less than two seconds. "Is he cute? Do you need help?"

For all Marian knew, there was another dimension out there where Bob and Vana hooked up. Well, it wasn't going to happen in this space-time. "Like I said, *my* future husband. Not yours."

* * *

Marian tried every door on the third floor until one of them opened. She rushed into the cluttered white room, shouting Bob's name. She heard a man's voice respond. She ran past a desk and tripped on a box of tools. She dove forward and tried to catch her balance. Her flailing arm caught several fluid-filled beakers on the counter and knocked them over. Her momentum took her toward the electric blue light of a laser cutting into a sheet of metal. Time seemed to slow as she fell. Her breath caught in her throat. She squeezed her eyes closed.

She didn't experience the searing pain she expected. Something collided with her from the side, knocking her off her feet. Arms reached around her waist and hoisted her onto unsteady legs. She looked up to find Bob—only he was about her own age. He stared down at her, out of breath. He was even dreamier than the older man she'd met, his face young and hair brown and held back in a ponytail. Forgetting he didn't know her, she touched the smooth edge of his jaw not yet tarnished by a pink scar.

He chuckled and cleared his throat. "It looks like I just saved your life, miss."

She pulled back, feeling confused. "That's not the way it was supposed to work. I was supposed to hurry over here so I could rescue you from a burning building."

He raised an eyebrow. "Who told you that?"

"A you from a different space-time."

He rubbed his hand over his unblemished jaw and shook his head. "Is that so? And you believed me? I hate to tell you this, but I think I may have set you up so I could rescue your life and make you fall in love with me. Did it work?"

Marian straightened her overalls, trying to hide her disappointment. "I don't think so." She glanced out the window, spotting the only lit room in the building across the street. Dr. Malachlor was no longer at his desk; he'd probably evacuated. He would be pretty ticked off to learn she'd interrupted his work for no reason.

Bob extended his hand. "Well, it's nice to meet you anyway. I'm Bob. It happens we're working on a time machine over here. I guess I was successful then?"

Marian stared at the half-built tower of junk piled up against the wall. It didn't look like much of a time machine to her. "Actually, I like to call you Bobby."

"Oh, no. I go by Bob."

"Well, um, nice meeting you." She shrugged and left, closing the door behind her. She held her head high, trying not to let her wounded pride show. Here she had thought she was finding her soul mate. This entire scenario had probably been some kind of prank. She doubted she even had a . . . what was it he'd told her was wrong with her? A brain tumor? A heart arrhythmia?

No sooner had she started down the hallway than something exploded behind her, rattling the entire building. Windows of the rooms lining the hall shattered. Marian raised her arms and turned away to shield her face from the burst of glass. Several lights went out. Dry wall and wood flew into the hallway.

A bolt shot into the hallway and skidded past her. Something whooshed by her head, thunking into the wall. She blinked. The hair brush she'd left back in the lab impaled itself halfway into the cream-colored surface. So the cold-fusion reactor had exploded. She wondered if that was what future Bob had meant when he'd said she had wished she'd taken the time to brush her hair—grabbing her hairbrush so it wouldn't nearly impale her. Or perhaps that was why he'd alluded to her taking her time getting there. He'd tried to change her fate from nearly being struck by a hairbrush, but time had turned out to be just as fixed as those moments when she'd been locked in the backwards pattern. All those dimensions he'd traveled to in order warn her about her future death, had it made a difference? Why hadn't he written it all down for her?

A thud and a strangled cry came from the room behind her.

The window of the door was broken. A warm glow emanated from inside. Marian raced back in, coughing from the smoke. The fluorescent light flickered before dying out completely, leaving the fire to light her path.

"Bobby?"

No reply. Something inside the supposed time machine was on fire. Pieces had fallen off. She edged around the corner of the counter, gagging from the fumes. A beaker of fluid on the counter popped, peppering her arm through her sleeve with glass. She screamed at the lightning jolt of pain. Momentarily, she staggered before forcing herself onward.

A gaping hole in the wall to outside gave her a ghastly view of the crater in her building across the street. The horror of it distracted her from looking at the debris at her feet. She almost missed Bob in the wreckage.

He lay face down. A metal coil from his time machine lay across his back. She grabbed the coil, but withdrew her hands as the metal seared her palms. Frantically she looked for something to use to move it. She found a lab coat to shield her hands as she threw it aside. Something else popped behind her.

There was no way she could carry him. And there was no way to grab his collar, turn him around and support his head in the enclosed space like they'd taught in that First Aid class. Trusting she'd done the same in future Bob's dimension, she grabbed his ankles and dragged him out into the hall.

Her heart raced so fast it felt as though it skipped beats, the pattern erratic. She placed a hand on her chest. What had he told her about her heart?

A whoosh of fire clouded out of the room, knocking her to the floor. It took a few seconds before she managed to stand and pull Bob to the elevator. Considering she couldn't drag him down the stairs without injuring him worse, she had to trust this was the choice she'd made in the other dimensions that had saved him. Once in, she pressed the ground button before dropping to his side. Immediately, she checked his pulse. It was steady, but she couldn't tell if he was breathing with the way he was remained face down. She rolled him over, but still couldn't tell.

Marian tilted back his chin and plugged his nose. As she pressed her mouth to his, he twitched and jerked his head to the side. A trickle of blood dripped from a cut on the edge of his jaw. It was in the same place future Bob had a scar.

He blinked at her. "Really, we've just met."

She laughed at that. "I've known you longer than you've known me at this point."

By the time Marian helped Bob stagger out of the elevator, the paramedics were in the lobby. They took over, questioning her about what had happened and asking if anyone else was inside. Her heart roared in her ears, drowning out the chime of the fire alarm. The erratic thumps sounded off. There was something about that. Something she couldn't quite remember.

"Oh, my god! Honey, are you all right?" Vana's voice was distant, even as she shook Marian. "My sister needs medical attention."

"Are you injured, ma'am? It looks like you're bleeding," one of the paramedics said.

Marian placed her hand on her chest, not sure if what she was feeling was love or something else. A poke of paper itched the inside of her bra. She slipped a hand under the collar of her overalls, pulling out a folded note. She opened it, reading Bob's reminder. The dizziness cleared from her brain.

"I need you to check me for a heart condition," she said.

Future Bob might not be able to return to his past to save her to create a different future for himself. But Marian was determined that in this dimension, she would have her quantum mechanic and a happy ending too.

Author's Note:

This story was an honorable mention in the contest for *On the Premises Magazine*, Issue #18. I love steampunk and this might have been my first steampunk story. It is a combination of my great genre loves: science fiction and romance. I always feel best when I get a happy ending . . . even if Pi is 3.2.

Red as a Pickle

The day the color red disappeared held little interest to Brigette the Cat. The color red dripped from packages of food dye, leached out of plastic toys, and dribbled off of tattoos, rolling like beads of mercury onto the floor. The humans stared in horror. Brigette glanced up from the dictionary she was studying—and shredding—then went back to the definition of "synergy." That annoying, yippy, mangy, flea-bitten, golden mutt she allowed her human pets to keep, gnawed his tail in nervousness.

"The world is going to end. It's a sign," he barked, repeating the words of other neighborhood dogs. Really, they were all so superstitious and well, dogmatic. Didn't Stupid Dog have an original thought of his own somewhere in his pea-sized brain?

By this point, it wasn't just Red Dye 40 that pooled onto the floor. The crimson of the coat in the closet wrung itself out like excess water, leaving the fabric white. The burgundy of Brigette's water bowl and the sanguine couch underneath her joined the crimson puddle on the floor. Maroon writing on boxes and the cherry red of markers blanched. Rose curtains lost their saturation. The tomatoes her human had painted in his still life turned gray. Splatters fell from the color wheel on the wall. The news broadcast Brigette allowed her humans to watch said infrared had ceased to exist. Whatever that was. All this chaos was ruining her nap.

The mass of color swirled around on the floor in a puddle. Her human pets screamed and ran from it. Stupid Dog tried to lick the liquid mass, but it moved too quickly and he got a hairball instead.

Brigette snickered at his oafishness. If she had wanted to catch the dancing ruby blob, she was certain she could have. But why bother herself to get up from the cushiony couch for a silly color?

The puddle found the crack under the front door and disappeared. Outside, the scarlet leaves shed their color. White sheets remained among gold and orange in the boughs. This vivid stream bled into the puddle and became larger. Red masses from other houses joined the growing river in the street.

Brigette examined her orange paw. The hair on her neck rose as she thought she might fade to the boring yellow of her dog servant. Being the master of human artists, she had uncommonly good color recognition—that and she was a cat and therefore nearly perfect in every way. She knew both red and yellow made up the orange of her fur. When her coat remained the same color, she decided not to question it too closely. She snuggled down on the now white couch and closed her eyes.

"The end of days is near. We have been punished for our wickedness," Stupid Dog said. "We are in a pickle, a real pickle. The Great Dog in the Sky is displeased with us, Sister Cat."

"Go back to chewing your tail. I need my beauty sleep."

Stupid Dog sniffed at the couch and licked it. "It doesn't taste the same."

Brigette extended her claws and waved them at the annoying dog yapping away. "Let's see if you still bleed red, shall we?"

* * *

Brigette sat at the window. Occasionally a blob of garnet jelly rolled down the street. It must have come from far away because there was no red for as far as she could see.

"Did you hear? Did you hear?" Stupid Dog panted. He still bore the claw marks marring his nose from the last time he'd annoyed her a week before. "The master has been talking about it! It was on the news! They think red might be returning."

Brigette twitched her whiskers. "Red is dead."

"No. It might be coming back." He chased his tail three times before he calmed himself enough to speak again. "A scientist was able to create the color in a laboratory. A scientist in another city."

"I didn't see that on the news." Brigette's curiosity was momentarily piqued. She did her best to squelch it. After all, she knew what they said about curiosity and what it did to cats.

"Well, the pickle is, they can't prove it. They created the color red but it melted away like the rest. But they did have it. They did! I heard the humans say so. Aren't you excited? We might find salvation after all."

"Shut up. I'm thinking."

Stupid Dog slobbered dangerously close to her whiskers. Dangerous for him, that is. Such an infraction was punishable by clawing.

"And you know what?" he said. "That red they created, rolled all the way here to our town. We're at the epicenter of the color quake. That's what the humans say."

She paced back and forth on the couch, digging her claws into the suede cover as she considered what all this meant. She hated it when trivial matters disturbed her. She settled herself down into the cushions of an especially tattered section of the couch, feigning her usual disinterest. "What do you care about any of this? Dogs are color blind." At least, they were blind to many of the colors she could see.

"I care because it's what the Great Dog in the Sky would want for us."

"That's rubbish." Brigette closed her eyes. Though she retained her cool, aloof exterior, her mind became more troubled than ever. Why had the color red disappeared in the first place? And why should she care?

Still, it vexed her that she did.

* * *

The day the color green disappeared, it started with the remnants of house plants that Brigette hadn't chewed. Leafy pigment dripped from the ferns hanging from the ceiling and drained to the floor. Her human pet leapt back. The avocado green refrigerator dribbled its hue into a puddle. The pickle one of her humans had set on the floor before Brigette paled. Though Brigette had an eccentric fondness for the tangy tart flavor, somehow it had changed. It no longer satisfied her taste buds.

Stupid Dog hid behind the couch. He howled when the viridian of his collar leached into the puddle. Brigette watched with helpless fury as the green fabric of her catnip-filled mouse toy blanched. She sank her claws into the carpet and yowled. First red disappeared. Fine. Even with her artistic training—mostly involving the shredding of

47

color wheels and gnawing on paintings she didn't like while studying them in-depth—a cat's eyes didn't see the full spectrum of red that a human's did, and it was no great loss to her. But green? Her favorite color was being stolen from her? She would not tolerate this.

"Come with me," she ordered Stupid Dog.

He obeyed as she exited out the pet door into the back yard. The color of grass slowly slipped away, leaving a sea of white and gray blades. Not acceptable. Dribbles of yellow green splattered from the bushes, slowly rolling under the fence.

"We are going to find out what is happening to our colors and stop it." She nodded to the dog-dug hole under the picket fence that the master hadn't yet found. "You are going to be my sidekick and bodyguard. Someone I can ask to jump into a pit of fire to save the world—should such a situation come up—so I don't have to."

"Sounds great." Stupid Dog panted. Drool hung in a thick glob from his chin. His tail ceased to wag. "But what if the colors have disappeared because it's the will of the Great Dog in the Sky?"

"Then we will throw him out of the sky." Brigette's claws distended as she thought what she would do to any dog should he mess with her colors. She leapt up onto the top of the fence.

Stupid Dog whimpered. She gazed down at him with contempt. As much as she wanted to hiss at him, she knew it would do little good. She had to think like a dog for a moment. She would rather have hacked up a hairball, but she imitated his narrow-minded reasoning anyway. "You think you will displease the Great Dog in the Sky. But what if the colors of our world are being stolen away and it isn't his doing? What if our enemies and his enemies are one and the same? We can do the bidding to the Great Mutt—err—Dog in the Sky by seeking out truth and saving ourselves from future color theft. This would bring you great honor. Wouldn't the stupid—err—Great Dog in the Sky be proud of you and want to honor you in the afterlife?"

Stupid Dog barked and chased his tail three times. "Amen, Sister Cat. Let's go chase a rainbow!"

Brigette fought the urge to barf. "I will wait for you on the other side." She leapt down from the fence and landed on the sidewalk. She eyed the river of rippling chartreuse and pine-green swirls flowing down the street. A car driving down the lane jerked over to the side to avoid the green river.

Stupid Dog dug his way under the fence and joined her.

"We need to stalk our prey. Sneak up on it with me." Brigette darted down the cracked sidewalk and hid behind a bush as white as snow.

Stupid Dog yapped and ran back and forth. He shouted loud enough for the entire neighborhood to hear. "I am an avenger of injustice. I fight evil and will bring color back to this world. For the good of all living creatures, I serve the Great Dog in the Sky."

The howls of every other dog in the neighborhood joined in his chorus of barking madness. Brigette groaned. So much for stealth mode.

* * *

Brigette considered what she would do if she did meet up with a Great Dog in the Sky—not that she believed in such a thing. But if it appeared in any way that a dog was responsible, she didn't know how she would get Stupid Dog to help her. Not that she thought a dog was bright enough to steal a color.

More importantly, she didn't know how she would be able to get color to return to her pickles and favorite catnip toy and all the other less important things in the world that humans liked. What if orange was next? Her beautiful coat would be gone. And where would the depletion of color stop? Would the world become a black and white tragedy?

Brigette stalked the river of green, noticing the way it seeped into the storm drains and grates in the street. She could easily squeeze through the slats in one of the bigger ones. Getting her bodyguard down was another matter.

"Maybe if I use my muscle," Stupid Dog said, trying to dig under the metal and lift it up.

"Maybe if you used your brain," Brigette said. She padded across the street, down another sidewalk and out of the neighborhood of newer houses. "But since you don't have one, you're going to have to do a better job of minding me. If I say, 'stealth,' that means no barking. If I say, 'Sic 'em,' that means destroy our enemies. Got it?"

He barked merrily, oblivious to the car accident at the stop light at the end of the street.

She passed smaller homes with quaint fenced yards that sloped downward on the hill. The trickle of water sounded close by. Beyond the chain link fences of the yards grew white-leafed trees lining a stream. Trails of olive and aquamarine descended into the gully below. She hadn't been this far from home since that one night she'd gotten in a fight with a feral tabby cat who thought she was queen of the neighborhood. Brigette had shown her otherwise. After their fight, Brigette had been so weak, she'd fallen down the slopping hill and into the stream. She had discovered the wide yawning pipe in the ground that the rain water poured into.

Brigette guided Stupid Dog to the pulled back area of the fence and made her way through the gray and white weeds along the banks of the stream. The algae-covered rocks were now pale. Globs of lime and pea green rolled over the trickling water and glided into the hole. Brigette jumped onto one rock and daintily leapt onto another. Stupid Dog thrashed in the water behind her, splattering cold water onto her coat.

He wagged his tail. "I had no idea saving the world would be so much fun."

She cast him a venomous glare. He didn't notice.

When the rocks ran out and the only choice was to jump into the stream of water washing into the darkness, Brigette considered whether she really cared about the color green. She didn't enjoy getting wet unless it came from a bath from her own warm tongue. Could she get used to pickles that were white? It was possible her orange fur was safe. But no, she had to go on. If she'd gone to the trouble of making a dog assist her and tracking the color into the stream below the streets, she might as well keep going.

She plunged into the watery shadows of the tunnel. Shafts of light from grates above illuminated sections of the shallow stream. She followed the labyrinth of tunnels as they slanted downward, away from the distant noises of automobiles and children playing. Her eyes adjusted to the blackness, following the trail of green blobs drifting by. Stupid Dog whined and stumbled into the walls as the darkness increased. The cold of the water chilled Brigette. The stream deepened. The only familiar sound was that of Stupid Dog snuffling and splashing. A rank, fetid stench wafted toward them.

The water grew so deep, Brigette lost her footing and crashed into Stupid Dog. Thrashing to keep her face above the surface, she sank her claws into the fur of his leg for support. "Save me, Stupid Dog! Don't let the water sweep me away."

He nudged her with his nose. "You're safe with me. Climb on my back."

Brigette did so. She licked a paw and pretended she hadn't nearly drowned.

"You know," he said. "My name isn't really Stupid Dog. The master calls me Ralph."

"You're unworthy to be called by a real name. You haven't earned it."

"So you might call me Ralph if I prove myself?"

"I suppose," she said.

The path forked up ahead. Blobs of green floated toward the right. Stupid Dog headed straight forward—toward the wall.

She tugged on his right ear. "Turn right, Stupid Dog." He turned in time to avoid crashing, though he still managed to scrape the side of his body against the wall, smooshing her paws.

"Boy, that's pretty swell you can see in the dark like that. We make a good team, you and me. Your brain and my brawn."

Brigette coughed up a hairball in reply.

At the next fork, she told him to wait. She saw no more green in the water. She shivered against the warmth of his back, hoping a bead of shimmering emerald would pass by so she might be able to see which direction to take. No color passed them.

"What are we waiting for, Sister Cat?"

"I can't see the color in the water anymore. We can't keep going until we know where it has gone."

He sniffed the walls and splashed at the water. It remained black and unreadable. Panic tightened in Brigette's fur-covered chest. Had they come all this way for nothing? Her sidekick sniffed at the air and turned to the right.

"What are you doing?" she asked.

"Can't you smell it? The perfume of limes? The musk of algae? The scent of plants and avocados and my dog collar?"

"Ahem, of course," Brigette said, not wanting to admit a mere dog could do something she couldn't.

Slowly he trailed down the tunnels, pausing every so often to sniff before moving on. Brigette noticed an odor in the air, but it wasn't the smell of green. It was the reek of sewage. She would have liked to stuff catnip up her nose to block it out. Her companion didn't seem to mind. Instead he commented on the rainbow of odors.

"I can smell cherries and red gum drops. Do you smell them?" he asked.

"Uh huh," she said.

What she did notice was the faint glow coming from up ahead. As they traversed the underground, she detected a hint of red reflected on the walls. A flicker of scarlet danced on the water. The tunnel grew brighter and she could see more clearly as it opened up into an immense concrete chamber. Jarring ruby and emerald light danced over the walls. The luminescence undulated in a mass before them. The swirls of light reminded Brigette of Christmas. In the center of the writhing sea of color were two shadowy forms bleeping and blipping in a tongue that sounded neither animal nor human.

"It's our enemies. The ones who stole color." Brigette hissed, her fur standing on end.

Stupid Dog bounded forward, dropping her from his back. His barks echoed in the chamber, alerting the shadows of their presence. Instead of dropping into the water, Brigette bounced onto the smooth chartreuse surface. Though the viridian ripples moved like water, it was packed so solidly she couldn't get her claws to sink into the concentrated mass.

The two hazy shadows ceased bleeping and hovered above Stupid Dog. They circled him before settling on a brilliant patch of red. Their insubstantial shapes solidified into the form of two large dogs. One shifted from black to red, the other to green. They both resembled the short-haired golden lab mix that made up Stupid Dog. Brigette hissed softly, knowing this was a bad sign.

Stupid Dog's gray tongue wagged out of his mouth in excitement. "Oh boy! Dogs! Just like me."

Brigette prowled at the perimeter.

"Greetings, Earthling," said the green dog in a clipped, foreign accent. It allowed Stupid Dog to sniff at it.

"What a beautiful color that fur is," the red dog said. "Might we inquire what you call such a hue?"

Stupid Dog glanced down at his paws. "This? It's yellow."

The two dogs exchanged glances and nodded as if they'd just agreed upon an important matter.

"No!" Brigette leapt across the marbleized colors. "You will not take yellow too. These are our colors, not yours. You need to put red and green back where you found them."

The two dogs exchanged glances again, the mocking aloofness of a cat reflected in their eyes. "Our world, so far away that it is but a speck in your sky, has no colors. We live on a planet of black and white. These gifts we have collected will be of great value to our people."

"You mean, you're Great Dogs in the Sky? There's more than one?" Stupid Dog asked.

Brigette raked her claws against the floor. Her chances of getting colors back seemed slimmer than ever.

"We will keep red and green," said the red dog. "And perhaps our world would benefit from yellow as well." The red dog tilted his head at Brigette and studied her orange coat.

Oh, no. They would not have that. Not if she had anything to say about it. She forced herself to remain calm. Right now she was outnumbered three to one. She had to think of a way to gain an advantage.

"What is that color called?" the green dog asked.

"Orange? No, no, please take my yellow coat," Stupid Dog said. "I wish to please the great dogs in the sky."

"All in good time. We'll take that next. Bleep blip blip!" They laughed.

Brigette shook Stupid Dog, who stubbornly continued to pant with his tongue lolling out of his mouth. "Don't you see, those aren't dogs?" She rounded on them. "You can do what you please, take any color you choose, no matter what we do, right? Then at least tell him the truth. You aren't dogs."

They returned to black shadows, red and green sparks of light sinking to the glowing ground. "We are from the sky above. We are all-knowing and all-seeing gods of the cosmos. We can take on any form we choose. But until now, we have had no colors but black and white. Now our power is complete."

Drool dripped from Stupid Dog's mouth. "Another world? In the sky? This is my dream come true."

"Look at them? Do they stink like dogs?" Brigette asked. "Do they slobber and wag their tails and scratch at fleas? They're trying to trick you."

Stupid Dog's head dropped between his shoulders. He pawed at the ground with uncertainty.

Brigette cast a glance at their enemies where they hovered just above the swirls of the floor. She had to make Stupid Dog see. She padded forward with more confidence than she felt. "They claim to be powerful. But are they? I mean, sure, they turned into dogs. But so what? Anyone can imitate a dog. Can they turn into something bigger? Something smaller?"

The two shadows joined together and grew, drawing in colors from the saturation around them. Brigette held her ground, not daring to back away and show weakness. The aliens sparkled with red and green as they grew into the shape of a tiger, melted into a horse, bloated into an elephant.

"As we said, we are all powerful."

Brigette groomed a paw. "It's always easy to grow bigger. A kitten can turn into a cat. A puppy into a dog. But can you grow smaller? Can you fit all that mass into something small? Into two, little . . . ahem, mice?" Her heart thundered as she said the words.

The elephant separated and shrank. Some of the saturation of color dropped away. Brigette tried to catch Stupid Dog's eye, but he stared so mesmerized she suspected she might be on her own.

Just as the two aliens turned into a red and green mouse, she shouted, "Sic 'em!"

She pounced, snatched up the red mouse in her jaw. Her teeth sank into the furry red form. It tasted of red licorice and roses.

"No, please, don't kill me!" it cried in a small, pathetic voice. She held it firmly in place with her teeth. She refrained from killing it just yet.

Her companion hesitated just long enough for the mouse to swell up to the size of a rat. Then he leapt forward, snapped it up and crunched into it. He shook it like he did when he caught a gopher in the yard. Then he bit its head off. Such an impulsive dog thing to do. It certainly hadn't brought any colors back.

The mouse in her mouth squealed. "Free me this instant. I am the Great Dog in the Sky."

Stupid Dog growled. "You don't look like a dog to me. I think you're a plain thief. Bite him, Sister Cat."

As difficult as it was to talk with her mouth full, she did. "I will free him if he promises to return all color to our world."

"No," the little voice said.

She sank her teeth deeper.

"Ow! All right."

The glowing brilliance underneath drained away from the ground and out into the tunnels. Slowly she sank lower as the colors receded, giving way to water. She scrambled into a tunnel, clinging to a small ledge off to the side. Stupid Dog bumbled into her. The glow of lime and scarlet receded away as they returned to the world.

"I've done as you asked. Now release me," said the mouse.

"Are you going to do it? Are you?" Stupid Dog asked, nudging her side with his nose. "The Great Dog in the Sky would want you to honor your word."

The alien was dangerous and cunning. It could easily steal colors again. Brigette didn't trust it any more than she did, well, another feline. She crunched down on the small form and swallowed.

"Fortunately for me, I'm a cat. I don't need to follow your code of doghood." She scrambled up onto her sidekick's back. "Now use your nose and get us out of here."

* * *

"They brought back color to the world. And then we ate them," Stupid Dog said to the humans sitting on the couch as if they understood. "It was ordained. We were doing the work of the Great Dog in the Sky."

Things were back to normal, more or less.

Brigette tolerated his company beside her on the lime green couch. She'd never permitted him to sit up there before, but she supposed his presence wasn't quite as odious as it once had been. He scratched at his red collar and she shifted away.

The male human pet rose from his seat and strolled into the kitchen. Brigette's ears perked up when she heard him open the pink refrigerator door.

"So, have I earned being called by my true name?" Stupid Dog asked.

She twitched her whiskers, watching her human pet reach inside the refrigerator.

"I suppose, Ralph." Saying it was akin to stabbing herself in the eye with his chew toy.

"Yay! You and me, we're such good buddies. What's your true name, Sister Cat?"

Glass grated against metal as the human opened the pickle jar. She leapt from the couch and padded over to the carpet. "You may call me the title the humans ordained me when I was a kitten: Princess Brigette Anastasia Mousekiller."

"Oh boy!"

The human crunched into a pickle. He set one down as an offering at her feet. It was brilliant scarlet.

They had brought back color to the world. More or less.

Author's Note:

As an art teacher, I am often thinking about colors. I read the first pages of this to one of my middle school classes and asked them to tell me what details in this world are fantasy and wouldn't be able to happen in our own world. *Bards and Sages* published this despite of, or perhaps because of, my fantasy take on color theory. I suspect my lack of color reality is made up for by my realistic representation of cat and dog personalities. Sometimes I have bad dreams about cats like this one.

Cinderella's Holo-wand

With a package under her arm, Kerri waited at the crosswalk while hover cars in the street rushed by. Her belly rumbled from skipping lunch, so she broke off a piece of chocolate bar in her pocket and nibbled on a few squares. Traffic slowed to a stop. A man on an old-fashioned motorcycle removed his helmet and looked her up and down. Her heart skipped a beat upon seeing his long black hair flowing behind him and his chiseled features. He smiled appreciatively.

Warmth crept into Kerri's cheeks. For a moment, she forgot she was forty-two, overweight, and wearing her blandest business suit. She thought he was eying her. She wanted him to be. The spell was broken when two teenage girls giggled behind her. They strode past Kerri, their fashionable mini-skirts showing off long, shapely legs.

The man's eyes flickered to her metal leg, pity flashing across his visage before he returned his helmet to his head.

Kerri rolled her eyes, disgusted at herself for thinking the model-gorgeous man could possibly be ogling her.

She limped across the crosswalk, her prosthetic leg slowing her down.

Kerri reasoned if it wasn't for her injury, she could look like those teenagers. Even when she did have time to eat healthy meals and go to the gym for more than two days during the week, trying to look like a normal woman was impossible with a hunk of metal attached to her thigh.

All that was about to change.

Breathless by the time she reached her apartment, Kerri held her hand up to the security pad. She shifted from foot to foot in impatience as she waited for the door to her apartment to unlock. Her fingers danced over the package she carried.

Kerri needed to start dinner and check her work emails before the board meeting that night. Still, she couldn't resist the urge to at least open her order from Holo Visions Cosmetics. Giddy as a child on Christmas morning, she tore through the tape with a pair of scissors. She sifted through the biodegradable peanuts and found the metal baton. Rows of buttons and dials lined the holo-wand. She plugged the adaptor into an outlet in the living room and pressed the on button.

A pleasant female voice announced, "Welcome to Holo Visions Cosmetics. In order to make the most of your purchase, please watch and listen to the new user orientation." A hologram rose in the air from the wand, blocking her wall screen and couch with the image of a beautiful woman on a tropical beach.

Kerri had already read the product manual and tested out the online version of the program. She knew exactly what she needed to do. She waved her hand in the air to swipe away the introduction. When the user agreement came up, she tapped her hand in the air against the "I accept" button and scrolled to the menu.

She selected the scan icon.

"Please remove all clothing for an accurate scan," the automated voice said.

Kerri threw off her clothes. She shivered in the chill of her apartment. She proceeded to wave the wand up and down in the air around her body, paying particular attention to the remainder of her mangled leg. Before her, an image of a human body materialized. She recognized the flat chest, flabby belly and unshapely thighs as hers, yet they looked so much more unsightly on a 3-D hologram than when she looked in the mirror. Worst of all was the void where the metal leg screwed into hers. A cross hatching of scars lined the lower half of her body. Her breath caught in her throat. Even after years of physical therapy and a dozen reconstructive surgeries, she never got used to seeing her injuries from the hover bus accident.

"Please move the wand slowly across the face for an accurate scan."

Kerri had no intention of reconstructing anything other than her leg. Still, she followed the program's instructions, noting the way the generic manikin came to resemble her with eyes that were a little too small and lips too thin to be aesthetically pleasing. The scanner captured her weak chin, thin brown hair streaked with silver, and the waddle under her chin. The computer saw through the layer of carefully applied makeup she wore to hide her wrinkles. It showed the truth of her imperfections.

Until recently, this technology had been used by doctors for creating replicas of burn victim's faces to guide reconstruction, and for plastic surgeons to demonstrate what patients might look like who underwent liposuction or breast implants. With the newest advancements in holo fields, it made such surgeries unneeded. For those who could afford it anyway. Having a good credit score like Kerri did meant taking out a loan was another option.

"For modifications, select the enhancement button," the computer-generated voice commanded.

Kerri turned the wand over, finding the glowing green button with ease. She loved how user-friendly the product was. A golden ring appeared around her avatar's middle. Kerri waved her hand over the halo, pushing it down to her legs. She scrolled through the options, selecting the one for symmetrical balance. The human avatar before her now looked whole, with two complete legs.

"Wave the wand over the desired area again to apply this selection," the computer voice said.

A holo outline flickered into view around the metal leg. The holo field tingled against her skin, causing goosebumps to rise on her flesh. She waved the wand over her prosthetic. The field filled in with her skin pigment and solidified. The goosebumps that had been on her bare thigh now reflected across her computer generated leg. She smoothed her fingers over the new knee and down to the ankle, amazed how real it felt.

Kerri tentatively stepped forward. She rolled onto the ball of her foot and back to her heel. The projection responded like it belonged to her. Tears filled her eyes and she laughed. For the first time in nearly twenty years, she felt like herself. She wanted to run. To jump. To do cartwheels and all the other things she hadn't been able to do since she was young. She could already feel how much more of a cushion this was on her stump. Best of all, no one was going to give her those pitying looks anymore.

"Are you finished with your alterations or would you like to implement additional changes to your body?" the voice asked.

Kerri eyed her avatar. She looked normal for her age, nothing special. She had sneered at the advertisements showing women erasing wrinkles and increasing their bust size. But now, with the holo-wand in her hand, she didn't think a test simulation would her hurt.

She glanced at the clock, amazed an hour had passed. She should have started dinner by now. Then again, she could heat up a frozen dinner and eat it as she reviewed the information for the board meeting they were having in a few hours. That would give her time to play a little longer.

She started with her flat chest, enhancing the size and then the shape. First, she went up a cup size and gave her breasts a lift. Curious what she would look like with double D cups, she had to try it.

She walked around the avatar, admiring the way her endowments made her flabby belly and lumpy thighs less hideous.

The wand said, "If satisfied with this selection, please press enter and wave the holo-wand over the area of the body requiring change."

Kerri did so, shivering as the holo field prickled against her bare flesh. Motion in her peripheral vision caught her attention. Looking past her only partially drawn curtains, an old man in the apartment next to hers stared, his mouth hanging open.

"Oh shit!" Kerri ducked out from his view and closed the curtains.

She checked the digital clock on the wall. She still had time to warm up a frozen dinner before getting ready for her meeting. It wasn't like she could wear these breasts to her work meeting. No one would take city council's proposal for the grant seriously if they were staring at her country-singer-sized chest.

On the other hand, staring at her more attractive self, she was compelled to see what she would look like without belly flab. After another hour of playing with her enhancements, her nose became long and straight instead of turned up. Her eyelashes transformed into long, black ones, contrasting against smooth skin as fair as porcelain. The holo field cinched her waist into an hour glass figure. The vivacious blonde hair flowing down her back had been a last minute touch. She posed and the avatar posed like a human-sized doll. If she walked out of her apartment looking like this, no one would know her. She could lead a secret life. She smiled at the idea of showing up to work and seducing that cute messenger boy.

The thought of work brought her back to reality. She glanced at the clock. She definitely didn't have time to make dinner and read emails. Then again, she could swallow a snack pill and have a real meal later. That would give her time to play a little longer. . . .

She selected a conservative, flowered dress from her walk-in closet. The research she'd done indicated that if she selected the fashion feature on the wand, her old clothes would fit her body while the holo field altered itself to mirror the clothes underneath. Amazingly it did so. When she waved the wand over the wrinkles in the fabric, they smoothed away as easily as they had over her face. Not yet satisfied, she changed the color of the dress to a solid red and flared out the skirt.

Only when she went to the back of the closet for an ancient pair of heels she hadn't worn in years, did she feel the holo field against her skin dissipate. She stumbled as her weight changed back to her prosthesis. She looked down to see her sagging breasts under her flowered dress. When she stepped out of the closet, the holo field prickled against her skin and the field around her waist constricted again. Backing up into the far corner, the field left her.

The reviews hadn't said anything about a limit to the range of the wand.

She called the menu back up in her living room. "What's the range of the holo-wand? It doesn't have a limited signal, does it?"

Kerri glanced at the clock. She had emails to read and data to print out before she left her house. But it wouldn't hurt if she just figured out this last detail.

There was a pause before the automated voice responded. "Would you like to know more about long distance usage?"

"Yes," Kerri said firmly so the computer wouldn't mistake her reply.

"Roaming charges cost an additional five hundred dollars a day."

Kerri swore at the machine. Of course, Holo Visions Cosmetics would think of a way to charge another arm and a leg. Another fee would dip into what she had left in her bank account. She'd saved that for rent. On the other hand, what good was it to have this body if she didn't take it out of the apartment?

"If you would like to pay the roaming fee, please have your credit card ready," the holo-wand said.

Kerri got it out. If she didn't read everyone's emails before tonight's board meeting, she wouldn't have all the information needed for the presentation. On the other hand . . . she could check her email from her phone on the way to city hall. Half an hour was all she needed. She could go back to playing with the holo-wand after the meeting. This wouldn't be like the time she got sucked into that i-fitness skydiving game and was late for work.

A holo-wand replica appeared in her avatar's hand. Her likeness demonstrated how to untwist the end to remove a metal ring the size of a large washer. White and green lights lit the piece.

"Please keep this antenna on you at all times." The ring became a fashionable amulet hanging on a silver chain around her avatar's neck. "If you would like to turn it off, twist it like so."

With a string she found in the kitchen drawer, she recreated the necklace around her neck.

She strode out her door with her smallest purse, determined to take a quick test stroll around her apartment building before heading back up. Her neighbors held the door for her at the elevator. Mr. Mitchells looked her up and down.

"Hello," Kerri said, wondering if they recognized her.

"Um, well, h-h-hello. Are you new here?" Mr. Mitchells stammered. His wife elbowed him in the ribs, her lips pursing.

Kerri giggled, feeling like a teenager. Though, not the teenager she'd once been with her mousy brown hair and pudgy baby fat.

She walked around the block, admiring the naked desire on men's faces. Sunlight glittered across her toned arms, drawing the stares of women as well. She passed by the athletic club, doing a double take at the leggy blonde that was her reflection. She couldn't help smiling at her sexier herself. She batted her extra long eyelashes. The motion beyond the glass caught her attention. Three attractive men lifting weights stood gawking at her. One of the men handed a dumbbell to his beefy friend, but the weight fell through his fingers onto the floor. He stared out the window. She didn't need to glance around to see what had distracted them; she knew it was her. She raised a hand and waved. One of the men sitting on the weight machine leaned forward.

Kerri blew him a kiss and winked at him. She would never have done such a thing normally. She laughed at herself. This is what it was like to be beautiful. She let her hips swing like Marilyn Monroe. She held her head high, meeting the eyes of men she passed and allowing a sultry smile to play across her lips. She could do anything she wanted in this mask.

At the end of the street, she stopped at the crosswalk, tempted to prolong her excursion a little longer.

A man in a hover car called out to her, "Hey, hot stuff! You need a date tonight?"

A motorcycle passed her, screeched and braked. Kerri stared at the twenty-first century vehicle. It was rare to see gas-fueled vehicles anymore except among collectors and this was the second one she had seen today. The helmeted rider turned his head over his shoulder to gaze at her. A hover car beeped behind him. The rider revved his engine, hopped the vehicle up onto the sidewalk, and pulled up beside her.

Kerri placed a hand on her hour glass waist and struck what she hoped was a sexy pose. She raised an eyebrow. He removed his helmet.

He was the same rider as before. His long mane of black hair wafted in the breeze. His leather motorcycle jacket was shiny and pristine. Even the imperfection of the scar across his cheek couldn't mar his romance novel handsomeness. His lips parted and his mouth worked like he wanted to speak but no words came out. This was the first time she'd ever seen such hunger in anyone's eyes for her. Especially not from an attractive man fifteen years her junior. Her heart fluttered.

He held out his hand to her. She took it, thinking he meant to shake it or kiss it. Instead, he tugged her closer and kissed her on the mouth. She'd never been kissed by a hot stranger. Granted, it was a little sloppy. Like her first kiss from Hal Reynolds when she was sixteen. But that probably just meant he was passionate; her beauty brought out a beast in him. Something about the idea of that stirred desire in her.

He broke away and with a wicked grin, handed her the helmet. She understood he wanted her to wear it. To ride off with him?

But the meeting. . . .She had responsibilities. Then again, to hell with it! Board meetings were for boring, ugly women. This was the new her. She deserved an adventure, damn it.

She put on the helmet and climbed behind him. Her heart raced as he whizzed into traffic, leaving the area of nicer apartment complexes and condos, passing high rises of shopping malls, and heading into the residential neighborhood of mansions.

Her insides quivered as she realized her holo body had attracted a handsome millionaire. This really was the best day of her life.

He parked the motorcycle in the middle of an empty drive way. She followed him up to the entrance. He pressed his palm against the security panel and hugged the other around her.

Kerri noticed how hard his belly was under her fingers. It was the washboard abs gym commercials advertised. Could she really be with a millionaire, body-building hunk? She pressed herself closer and kissed him. Again, it wasn't very good, but it had been four years since she'd gotten laid, so she didn't think she should be picky about minute details.

He led her up a winding staircase, their footsteps echoing in the empty mansion. He pushed through a door covered with a poster of a basketball player. Inside, there were more posters on the wall. On one side of the room was a twin-sized bed, on the other side was a desk and chair. Sports equipment peeked out from a closet. A science textbook sat on top of a stack of other books next to a backpack.

Kerri hesitated. This was a kid's room. This guy had to be married. She glanced down the hall at the other closed doors. Did he have a wife behind one of them?

He tugged her hand, leading her to the bed. He let his jacket fall to the floor and unbuttoned his jeans.

Kerri cleared her throat, uncertainty creeping over her. "I don't even know your name."

"Mickey," his voice came out high and child-like. He cleared his throat and coughed. He said his name again in a deep voice that was obviously fake. Kerri saw the holo ring on the chain around his neck. At once she understood.

She grabbed it and twisted. The grad school-aged hottie disappeared. A scrawny young man with his jeans around his ankles stood before her. The stubble that had been on his face was replaced by smooth, youthful skin. The scar was gone, as was the long hair. It was unlikely he was even sixteen.

His youthful face affected her like a sucker punch in the gut. She struggled to breathe. Her thoughts raced with horror. She'd almost had sex with a minor? With a kid! How could she have been so stupid?

No wonder he was such an inexperienced kisser. He hurriedly yanked up his pants.

The shock on his face gave way to shame, then anger. Kerri backed toward the door. She reached under her collar and held up her own holo disk. With a twist, she returned to her former self.

His high voice cracked. "Oh, my god!" He made a retching noise.

Kerri turned away and stumbled down the stairs. The metal of her prosthetic limb clanked against the floor. Her eyes filled with tears. This was the most humiliating day of her life. She couldn't believe she'd been so stupid. She checked her watch. Ugh! She was late for the board meeting. Her heart raced as she came crashing back to reality. What the hell had she been thinking? She needed to check her emails. She wasn't going to get the grant. She should call someone and tell them she ran into traffic.

And she needed to return the holo-wand.

Kerri ran out the door and panted as she limped down the sidewalk. Another two blocks and she would probably find a hover taxi with ease.

A holo billboard in the sky shimmered with a Holo Vision Cosmetics advertisement. Her heart lurched in her chest when she saw the words: "The Holo-wand 2 is available now! No roaming fees!"

Author's Note:

The inspiration for "Cinderella's Holo-Wand" came from an occasion when I was wearing a costume for a belly dance performance that included a wig, a tutu-like dress and false eyelashes. I always feel so glamorous, like another person, when I wear false eyelashes. It is like a mask and I am transformed to someone else—a stage persona. I happened to be walking down the street and I saw a reflection of myself in a glass building in this costume. As I was admiring myself, I realized the men inside the gym beyond the window panes were staring at me and must have thought I was looking at them. As my normal self I am shy and mousy, but in the costume as this other self I winked and blew them kisses, transformed into a starlet. I kept thinking about the idea of transformation and being someone else for several weeks after that incident and wrote this story. It was published by *Perihelion Magazine*.

The Optimist Police

Tony had done a good job faking optimism most of his life, but recently with the new surge in Optimist Force technology, he'd been caught twice. The first time at a restaurant, the second in a theater. As if the acting in the movie hadn't been bad enough to ruin his date, the police trampling over theatergoers to get to him wasn't exactly a romantic way to end the evening.

"Happy thoughts," Tony muttered as he walked along the street of boutiques and specialty shops. "Happy thoughts, happy—don't let them catch me. Happy—Oh, shit, did I turn off the oven?" He pushed a handful of his black hair away from his itching eyes, took a deep breath and sneezed. Damned allergies. Why did there have to be so many trees in this stupid city? He'd woken up to hay fever, failed to deliver two pizza's within the forty minute time limit while at work, and now he had to go to his thirtieth birthday party and see his annoying family. This was the shittiest day ever.

A siren sounded the next street over. Tony quickened his pace, hoping to lose himself in the crowd of Saturday shoppers on the street of trendy little shops. He could still get those cannoli shells from Pastaworks if he hurried.

A large man blocking the sidewalk in front of Tony exclaimed in a cloying voice, "What a beautiful day we're having!"

Tony glanced up at the typical, overcast Oregon sky. A raindrop plopped on his nose. "Don't say it," he told himself. "Don't look at them . . . think happy . . . singing in the rain. . . ."

"Mommy, I stepped in dog poo!" said a little girl of about seven. She crinkled up her nose in disgust.

Tony smiled in spite of himself. At least children thought like normal people.

"Worse things do happen," chirped the mother.

"Yeah, I'm lucky I didn't slip in it. I'm lucky I didn't get struck by lightning. I'm lucky I didn't have to take a math test."

They sounded like robots programmed for happiness. How did they do it? Even children made positive thinking sound simple.

Tony looked around. Police officers pushed through the crowd.

"Zippidy do da," he said. He tried to whistle, but his mouth was dry and he was out of breath.

They were going to catch him again, and this time he'd probably be sent to work in a coal mine.

"Blip blip bleeeeeeeep," the police scanners sounded as they approached.

Damn it, he had to stop doing it. Just keep his thoughts light and happy and their scanners wouldn't pick up any readings from his "pessimist chip," and they'd pass him by. If he was lucky.

Beeeeeep beeeeeeeeep.

"There he is!" shouted a police officer from up ahead. He pointed straight at Tony.

The other shoppers on the sidewalk shrank back as if he might infect them.

"It's one of them!" a man said.

A woman yanked her son away. "Don't let him come near my child."

Tony would have rolled his eyes had the circumstances been different. But at the moment, he was more concerned about being caught . . . again. Tony raced through the parting sea of people toward the Super X-Mart down the street. Two police officers were closing in. Tony ran across a street, dodging oncoming traffic.

"Shit! I'm going to get myself killed," Tony said as a car swerved out of the way.

Beeeep beeeeeeeeeeeeep a nearby scanner sounded.

Tony ran in front of another car that slammed on the breaks.

"You're lucky I didn't hit you!" yelled the driver.

Tony ran into the giant grocery store, hoping to hide. He looked up. Oh shit, they had surveillance cameras. Tony snatched up a basket, slowed his pace and tried to breathe deeply and clear his mind, just like they'd taught him to in the required optimist classes he'd taken in school. He paced the diaper aisle where he could be alone for a moment.

Breathe in unicorns and flowers . . . breathe out yucky, bad thoughts . . . breathe in rainbows and Armani suits . . . breathe out negativity. . . .He sneezed. Damn those allergies.

Somewhere nearby a scanner approached. Blip blip beeeeep.

If only optimists hadn't taken over the country after the war and required citizens to—No, he wasn't going there. Happy, happy. Attracting positive energy. Like attracts like.

"I am the architect of my own freakish universe," he said, plastering a smile on his face.

"Good for you, dear."

He whirled around to find an elderly lady placing a package of Depends in her cart. A police officer walked by the aisle, staring into the monitor of his hand-held pessimist monitor.

Blip blip blip.

Bunnies and snowflakes. Chocolate and cigarettes imported illegally from New Los Angeles.

The police officer passed the aisle.

Tony casually rounded a corner, placing more distance between him and the officer. He picked up a box and stared intently at it, trying not to look guilty. Laxative, now in mint flavor. Too bad he hated mint.

Bleeeeep.

He had to think of something happy fast. He wasn't constipated. He didn't need laxative. That was positive, right?

The police officer passed by, stopping briefly in front of a grumpy looking elderly man with five boxes of the laxative in his cart. How he didn't set the radar off, Tony didn't know. He probably was excluded from the optimist policy due to age.

While the police hunted him, there was only one place Tony could slip into oblivion and be free of all thought: the electronics section where he could watch television. It wasn't far, just past the books. That was a positive thought, right? He could do this. He usually did okay. It was just that he'd had a crappy—no, he wouldn't go there. He was doing a great job. He could be an optimist.

Tony strolled over to the TVs. A presidential speech blared from the loudspeakers. It wasn't the MTV he'd hoped for, but at least he liked the newly elected president. See, there was a positive thought.

"We've been plagued by one kind of terrorism or another for over a hundred years. It's about time we stopped it," came the president's southern drawl. The elected president was cloned with the popular traits of previous presidents; George Washington's face, George Bush's voice and Ronald Reagan's brain. Though with their luck, Ronny's brain would be post-Alzheimer's.

An alarm went off in the store. Fuck, he'd just done it again. He had to think of something optimistic. At least . . . at least the current president was better than . . . than . . . the Arnold Schwarzenegger, J. Edgar Hoover and a pit bull mix like the last one.

The siren stopped. Okay, mindless TV. He stared at President Wa-Bu-Gan's lips.

"With today's technology, we don't need to rely on telephone tracking or the internet to find our terrorists. We can receive messages from the chips implanted in a suspect's brains and monitor his thoughts. When words like 'can't,' 'won't,' 'shouldn't,' 'just my luck' and other pessimistic phrases come up, it will alert the Optimist Force. This, ladies and gentlemen, is your tax dollars at work."

A roar of applause erupted from the loudspeakers. Tony scratched his head. Hadn't the president been talking about terrorists a moment ago? Terrorism was supposed to be a safe topic he could agree with.

Blip blip bleeeeeeep.

Tony jumped, expecting to see an officer. No one was there.

Ring, ring, riiiiiiiiiing. Oh, it was his cell phone. What a relief. That was one optimistic thought right there.

Tony flipped the phone open. "Hello?"

The unmistakable Italian accent of his mother crackled over the cell phone. "*Bambino*, have you picked up *mia* cannoli shells yet?"

It grated on his nerves to hear her peasant dialect of Italian. The way she confused masculine and feminine was like the Ebonics of Romance languages. "Um, no, not yet, Ma. I, ah, had to make a detour." He backed away from the TVs to hear her response. There was an advertisement for the newest Disney movie, *Bambi's Mother is Resurrected*. It looked better than the last remake, *Eeyore's Happy Day*.

"I hear music. You at a strip club?"

Tony ground his teeth. "No, I'm at the grocery store." He backed farther away from the TVs. "Now really isn't a good time. Can I call you back when—"

"Your brother's coming over for dinner and bringing the kids so we need at least three more boxes of cannolis."

"How many cannolis are you making? That's eighteen more." Tony glanced over his shoulder. He might be able to make it to the parking lot exit and then slip down the street to Pastaworks. He shuffled toward the door.

"There's never too many cannolis. I'll pay you when you get here."

"Ma, I don't need you to—"

"Your brother makes more money than you, so he'll—"

Tony dodged behind an aisle to avoid a police officer. "Ma, I can—"

"If you could only get a decent job that wasn't at a pizzeria. Maybe you should pick up four more boxes instead of three. I have to make two different kinds. The batch with vanilla for Lucia's family and the kind with almond for everyone else. Oh, and I need to make some without eggs for Maria. She's always complaining about a—"

How could Tony not be a pessimist with a family like that? He didn't know how his brothers and sisters did it. His parents only escaped persecution because they met the age cut-off for the Can't-Teach-An-Old-Dog-New-Tricks Amendment. That, and they thought in Italian.

"—and I know your Uncle Guido is going to bring that *bruta puzzolanda, scuvosa—*"

Tony ignored the insult about his uncle's girlfriend. He was doing incredibly well considering who he was talking to. Maybe it was because his mother was the one doing all the complaining. He could see how the Optimist Force got so popular with people like his mother tainting the country.

Tony peeked around the aisle. He didn't see any officers. Slowly, he continued toward the exit.

"Spill on aisle three," said a voice over the loudspeakers, masking what his mother said. It was kind of nice actually. Hmm, there was another positive thought.

"—*de matsa vase. Pensa soltanto al sesso,*" she ranted in Italian.

"Uh huh, Ma. That's nice." Wait, did she just say he was always thinking about sex?

"I shouldn't even bother making cannolis. No matter what, they won't taste like *mia* mama's."

Tony glanced over his shoulder. The coast was clear. He was going to make it. Then he stepped into a puddle of oil. Tony slipped, but caught the edge of a shelf and stopped himself from falling. He even managed to hold onto his cell phone. He pulled himself upright. He was lucky. See, that was a good thought.

"*Che cosa è il punto*? I don't know why I try."

"Ma, I gotta—" Tony slid forward into a police officer.

"Excuse me, sorry about that. Good thing neither of us fell," Tony said.

She smiled and nodded before staring back at her radar. Tony beamed. He wasn't even a blip on her screen. He was doing great! And he could see the exit. He was almost there.

"You aren't even listening to me, are you, Antonio?" came his mother's voice from the phone.

"Uh huh. I really should—"

"This is what I get. I sacrifice the best years of my life and this is how you return *mia amore*. *Il mio bambino è una poca merda*. I should have called your brother to—"

Tony passed the registers. The door was just a few yards away now. "Ma! I am not a little shit." Why did she always have to compare him to his brother? He wouldn't be such a pessimist if he had a normal family. "And by the way, *amore* was masculine, not feminine. So it would be *mio amore*—"

Bleeeeeeeeep.

Fuck.

Five officers leapt onto Tony and pinned him to the ground. Within seconds he was handcuffed and being led toward a police car.

"Coming through. Nothing to see, folks," one of the officers said. "Just keeping this country safe from the invisible evils of pessimism."

* * *

Hours later, Tony sat strapped to a chair in a windowless room. The wires taped to his chest sent feedback to screens that were surrounded by men and women in lab coats. The only thing he could see from the chair was the large monitor that displayed spikes in his brainwaves indicating fluctuations of negativity.

An optimist technician whispered to a colleague, "Class C pessimist."

Whatever that meant, it wasn't good. As if being a third time offender wasn't bad enough. Another spike rose on the monitor.

"He has a ninety percent negativity rate for his thoughts," a woman in a lab coat said, shaking her head. "You know what happens to offenders like him."

A man in a black suit strode into the room. The optimist technicians retreated, fear in their rabbit-like eyes. The restraints on Tony's arms seemed to tighten.

The agent stopped in front of Tony and shook his head. "It's scum like you who jeopardize the optimist mission of peace, prosperity and goodwill. Conservative optimists are hoping to pass laws that will give us the power to execute criminals like you. Until that day, those bleeding heart liberals have alternative measures protecting your rights."

Tony let out a nervous giggle. See, he still had some rights. Though from the way the man's eyebrows came together and the deviousness of his smile, Tony couldn't guess what those rights were. He'd heard of criminals being sent to Alaska to work in mines, oil refineries, or on chain gangs. He hated the cold.

"We've tried rehabilitation and shock therapy for some . . . but you don't strike us as one a jury would elect for those programs."

Wasn't that sort of . . . a pessimistic statement? Maybe it didn't count if the man was smiling.

The technicians removed the wires and monitors from the room. One of them unfastened the straps on his arms, though not the ones on his legs. Tony rubbed his wrists.

"You have a choice. You can try your luck in the court system . . . or we can deport you."

Tony took in a sharp breath, imagining the worst; some place just as rainy and abysmal as Oregon—if there was such a place. After a long silence, Tony found the courage to ask. "Where will I go?"

"Our current relocation program is outside the country in the penal colony of California. You'll be shipped to New Los Angeles. The weather isn't the beautiful overcast we have here, and they don't have as many of the scenic forests of the Pacific Northwest, but we're confident you'll eventually adjust."

Was this a joke? Everyone normal liked sunny weather. And there weren't forests of pollinating allergens in New L.A.

"You won't be allowed contact with your family. We don't want you to influence the positive residents of this country. . . ."

Again, was this supposed to be a bad thing? He'd never have to pick up cannoli shells or listen to broken Italian again. They were testing him.

"You will have to continue your current occupation unless you request to change occupations with their government. . . ."

What? No digging up sewer lines or working on a chain gang?

The man snorted in disgust. "The people in New L.A. think of themselves as realists. They complain and cast their negative thoughts on others, worry about the future, and create their bad luck with their pessimistic thoughts. They can wallow in their self-loathing as they sit drunk in bars that don't have rules against smoking in buildings. They get what they deserve. . . ."

Yes, golden beaches and gorgeous women in bikinis, sunny and warm weather, palm trees, gorgeous women in bikinis, lots of good Mexican restaurants, freedom of thought and . . . gorgeous women in bikinis. Tony sighed with longing, wishing he were there already.

The man watched him, eyes narrowing. Tony slouched and pretended to look downtrodden.

An attendant walked into the room, carrying a portable pessimism detector. She whispered something to the agent.

Tony caught part of what she said. "—Our scanners indicate an unusual amount of optimism . . . possible candidate for shock therapy."

The agent nodded. Tony didn't want shock therapy. He wanted golden beaches and blonde women with little to no clothing. He wanted New L.A. He tried to think of pessimistic things fast. He'd be stuck in Portland forever, have to put up with his family, be haunted by these constant social-political pressures, and never have the chance to drink good tequila. He'd be miserable for the rest of his life, dreaming of what he'd almost had. He tried harder. If he was shipped off to New L.A., he would probably miss his family even if they were annoying. They'd probably relocate all the good-looking, bikini-clad women elsewhere right before he arrived.

Blip blip bleeeeeeeeep. The palm-sized machine sounded in alarm at his pessimist thoughts. The woman pressed a few buttons. "Oh, wait. I'm getting a reading. We must have been out of range. The technology is still fairly new. Sorry about that, sir."

The man grunted. Tony sighed in relief. He just had to stay completely negative a little longer. How was he going to be able to do this when he could almost taste the margaritas and illegal cigarettes?

The man's cell phone rang and he turned away from Tony, speaking with expressionless monotone. "Oh goody. Now that they've revoked the Can't-Teach-An-Old-Dog-New-Tricks Amendment, I'll be able to spend countless hours convicting more low-life pessimists."

A chill slid down Tony's spine. That was the law that kept people like his parents from being deported for their negative thoughts. What did that mean for people like him? Would he still be allowed to be deported?

The man snapped his phone closed and eyed Tony. "By the way, it takes about nineteen hours by bus to get to New L.A. You're going to be taking Greyhound. With your mother."

Tony sank back into his chair and groaned.

The pessimism detector from the other room beeped louder than ever.

Author's Note:

"The Optimist Police" originally appeared in *New Myths*. I started the story before I left for Japan after watching *The Secret* at a gathering with friends. Although I heartily agree with the concept of being the architect of your own universe, positive thinking and deciding what you want so you can make your own fate, I also got tired of the unrealistically optimistic viewpoint in many New Age-like teachings. This was one of my first parodies. It remained in a little booklet in one of my purses until I found it one day and read it to my mother while she was visiting me in Japan. At that moment as I was reading to her, I realized I wasn't much different from my five-year-old self who also wrote stories and read them to my mother.

Incidentally, my mother is also Italian-American and has sent me to the store to buy more cannolis.

You Say Potato, I Say Holy Crap

My mother eyed the celery on the cutting board with suspicion. Her weathered face crinkled up further with disapproval. The hint of an Italian accent flavored her words. "Are you sure this is organic? Celery's got more *pesticidas* than other *vegetales*. I don't see a sticker on it. I don't want to get one of them *accidentale* "Singing Celery" they cross with mocking bird DNA like they talk about in *miei maggazinos*."

"Organic, I promise," I said. It had cost double the normal price, too. And I'd had to buy it at some little hole-in-the wall fruit market that you could only get to by car, not hoverboard.

I wiped my just-washed hands onto the red ruffles of my apron as she inspected the other ingredients for the potato salad; omega-3 eggs, onions and basil with the organic label, Miracle Whip—instead of mayonnaise—and the potatoes. She'd been very clear that if I wanted her secret "Italian" potato salad recipe, I had to buy very specific ingredients.

She lifted a russet potato. "These are non-GMO *potatas*, no?"

I wasn't exactly sure what brand it was she didn't like, but I had looked for their label in the store and none of them said, "GMO."

"You got to make sure you don't eat GMO *potatas*. I read that they're crossed with a meat jacket and *porco* parts." She threw a dash of salt over her shoulder like she'd just uttered some Italian curse, then set the pot of water to boil at the electric stove.

"I think you mean a protein coat from a virus and bovine cells." I realized now, that by GMO, she must have been referring to genetically modified. "You can't believe all the crap you read in women's magazines. Half of it has no scientific basis. People have

76

been creating hybrids and genetically modifying foods for thousands of years." I nodded at my mother's half-Chihuahua, half-Siamese cat panting at her feet that she'd insisted on bringing over. "I mean, you wouldn't have Brutus if it wasn't for hybrids."

"There's a difference. We don't eat dogs."

"Not in this country."

She smacked me with her wooden spoon. "You've got to use the good peelers, not those *di merda* plastic ones."

I picked up a knife instead of my crappy plastic peeler, hoping this would appease the cooking diva in my kitchen. Smoothing my thumb over the surface of the potato, I noticed how warm it was in my hand. The skin was mapped in brown wrinkles, as weathered as an old woman's face. It gave just enough that it felt like I was squeezing a plump arm. The spots on the skin where eyes might grow looked like the liver spots on my mother's arms.

Was that the potato throbbing in my hand, or my own heartbeat I felt?

Brutus tilted her head, tail wagging. When I sliced into the potato, a miniature mouth with teeth opened up and screamed like a fabled mandrake root. Those teeth chomped down painfully on my thumb and I shrieked, dropping the potato. The cat/dog growled and barked at the rolling lump on the floor while my mother swore in Italian. She threw salt over her shoulder again and spit on the floor, probably to ward off evil potato spirits.

"*Merda!* See, I told you!" she shouted over the dog and potato.

Next time I would listen to my mother.

Author's Note:

I can't remember the original title for this story, but someone at my critique group suggested, "You Say Potato, I Say Holy Crap." At the time I was thinking a lot about genetically modified food and my Italian-American mother's potato salad recipe.

Interstellar Tech Support

Jonah Hubbard slowed his mini-pod as he passed Mars. His senses came crashing back to him as he exited hyperdrive. In the upper right hand corner of his visor, a red signal flashed, warning him his bullet-shaped, mini-pod leaked fuel. Had he been hit by the alien cruiser he'd passed right before he'd made his hyper jump out of the Reynolds Colony? His heart still raced from the encounter. Most humans who came in contact with alien vessels didn't live to tell the tale.

Earth twinkled like a star in the distance. So close, but not close enough. Jonah had few options left. He continued to Earth and flipped on the link to Rom Colonies Tech Support.

"Tech support, do you read? Tech support, come in," Jonah said into the microphone attached to his flight suit. His voice rose on the edge of panic when no one immediately answered. He forgot about the slight delay as his audio was sent through relay stations outside hyperspeed points.

"Hello, this is Rom Colonies Inc. Tech Support. To whom am I speaking?" an overly cheerful female voice asked.

"Jonah Hubbard. I'm having an emergency. I'm running out of—"

"Can I get your make, model and identification number to verify it's you, sir?"

Jonah clenched gloved hands, trying not to groan. "A T Class Bullet Pod. I need you to hurry. I'm running out of fuel." He couldn't detect leaking fluid when he craned his head to see out the glass bubble around him, but it was likely the leak was underneath his ship.

There was a pause before she responded. "Please hold as we verify your information." Pause. "Your warranty is nearly up. Would you like me to renew your policy?"

"No!" Jonah nearly screamed into the microphone. "I don't have time for that. I want to speak with a real human being who can give me tech support."

There was another pause. "Please hold for a moment as we connect you to the representative who can best serve your needs."

Annoyingly mellow music played over the intercom. Jonah pounded a fist against his dashboard.

"Hello, this is Prang. Can I get your make, model and identification number?"

Jonah took a deep breath and repeated his information.

"Thank you, sir. How can I help you today?" The female voice was just as cloying and mechanical as the last, only this time with a slight accent he couldn't place.

"My pod is leaking fuel," he said. "The nearest planet to land is Earth but I don't think I'll make it. I need help."

Pause. "Your warranty is about to expire. I would highly recommend you renew your policy. Would you like to do that right now?"

"Goddamn it! I need help. I don't know if those aliens will follow my hyper trail." Jonah ran a scan to check again.

Pause. "Excuse me, Mr. Hubbard. Did you say . . . aliens?"

"Yes. They might have shot me." Nothing showed up out of the ordinary on the screen in front of his chair. He waited for her response.

"Can you tell me exactly what happened so I can best help you?"

Jonah took a deep breath and recounted his situation. With her guidance, he sent a transmission of the last thirty minutes of system activity.

"Excuse me for a moment as I report the sighting of aliens to the United Planets," she said in her polite tone.

"But I need to—"

The droning melody signaled he was on hold. He clenched and unclenched his fists, wanting to pull out his hair—not that he could with the helmet encasing his head. He detested the hoops he had to jump through to get tech support. Not that other service providers were much better. Still, he couldn't help wishing he'd gone with Della Interplanetary Tech Support.

"Mr. Hubbard?" the voice on the line asked. "You don't have a leak. Your ship just thinks it does. You've been infected by an alien virus. Fortunately, that's covered under your service plan."

Jonah rolled his eyes. All Rom Col cared about was making money. If this was an issue not covered by his plan, they'd probably make him fork over another hundred credits for an upgrade.

"As soon as you land, we need to run a virus scan on your ship and reinstall piloting software."

That sounded pretty complex. It was the kind of thing he wouldn't be able to figure out on his own. Maybe his subscription to Rom Col Tech Support wasn't such a bad thing.

"In the meantime, you need a system reset. The first thing you need to do is reboot your ship," she said.

He turned off the engine. The consoles and panels in the cramped space around him immediately went dark. The vibrations of the motor stilled. Carried by momentum, his ship still headed toward Earth, but slowed.

The screen of his helmet still showed diagnostics. A red light in the upper right of his vision shield signaled the approach of a vessel leaving Earth's moon. He held his breath, hoping tech support might have sent message out to the U.P. and someone was coming to collect him. But he knew no interstellar vessels were likely to be out near the abandoned Earth colony besides an Earth artifact collector like himself. The U.P. would never spare a military class ship to save one civilian. Even so, he wanted to believe someone was about to rescue him if tech support failed.

Jonah clenched the controls in his gloved hands to stop the shaking. "Um, Miss . . . can you get a reading on that ship?"

"I'm unable to connect to your ship's monitors unless you link it over to me. I would like to take a moment to ask you again if you would like to renew your warranty. It's about to expire. Once it does, my company won't be able to assist you."

He used his suit controls to zoom in on the approaching vessel outside his window. It wasn't one vehicle. It was three blue spheres. His heart lurched. "Saturn's rings! Aliens! I don't have time to renew my warranty. You've got to get me out of here. Now!"

"Is that a no? I'm sorry to hear that, Mr. Hubbard."

"Now! I said now!"

Even without magnification, the blue dot glowed in the distance.

He stared in transfixed horror. It took him a moment to notice the tech support person hadn't said anything in response.

"Hello?"

There was no answer. He opened the monitor on his visor screen with his motion-controlled glove. The comm link was dead. He redialed. The wait was unbearable.

The same cheerful, AI voice as before came on. "Hello, this is Rom Colonies Inc. Tech Support. To whom am I speaking?"

"Jonah Hubbard. I'm having an emergency. I'm running out of f—"

"Can I get your make, model and identification number to verify it's you, sir?"

He rubbed at his helmet with his hands, unable to wipe away the trickle of perspiration on his face. "A T Class Bullet Pod. Hurry. My ship is out of fuel—err has a virus that makes it think it's out of fuel. Aliens are coming. I got disconnected." He gripped the armrests as he waited for a response.

The voice said, "Please hold as we verify your information." Pause. "Your warranty is now up. Would you like me to renew your policy? Please have your Galaxy Express Card number ready."

"Aaaaaarrrrrg!" Jonah screamed into his mic.

He fumbled through the zipped pouch next to his chair. Aside from a nutrition bar, a tissue and his wallet with cash in it, it was empty. He didn't have his Galaxy Express Card with him.

The ships were larger. They would be there in seconds. Would they shoot him immediately? Take him onboard and probe him?

He gasped for breath, feeling as though he were suffocating in his space suit. What could he do? Tech support wasn't going to help him. Money and upholding policies were all they cared about.

He thought about his friends and family that he would never see again. He considered what a waste of his time it had been dealing with tech support for the last fifteen minutes. Fifteen precious minutes of life that he could have used to call home and tell his girlfriend he loved her.

With a sudden realization, he saw it was fifteen minutes he could have used to get out of there. His ship wasn't leaking fuel; it was just a warning light that made it look like he was. He could still jump. Though, if he did, they were close enough to follow his hyper trail for certain. He didn't want to lead them home to Alpha Ryan II. He needed to get somewhere safe with weapons and reinforcements.

The aliens were almost close enough to fire at him. Jonah switched his ship back on. He set his hyper drive coordinates for the asteroid where Rom Col Tech Support and services were located. The alien ships would follow. Rom Col might not provide aid to him without a contract, but he was certain their security would be able to contain a flock of alien vessels if they had to protect themselves. A single space pod would be overlooked by the aliens with all the laser beams aimed at them. And if Rom Col couldn't protect themselves, well, Jonah didn't exactly feel bad.

Either way, after this, he would be switching to Della Interplanetary Tech Support.

He pressed the engage button.

Author's Note:

I have had so many bad experiences with my own version of Rom Colony Tech support. I bought a laptop from a major computer company and was supposed to get a $200 discount with my mail-in rebate and the company didn't honor it, nor were they as eager to assist over the phone since there wasn't an opportunity to sell me a product. When I lived in Japan, the hard drive on this same American laptop died. Several times it crossed my mind when writing this, "Dude, you're getting a dud." Though I didn't include that line in the story, it circled like music in my brain since that was the company's slogan in commercials—sort of. This story was a compilation of every tech support experience I had with a science fiction happy ending—for me anyway. *Penumbra Magazine* originally published this story in 2014.

The Last Supper

Seven things I was certain of when I woke up Thursday morning to make Thanksgiving dinner:

1. Yams are supposed to sit in a dark pantry until used so they don't sprout. They shouldn't glow with an eerie green light. Ever. If they do, that serves you right for not buying organic.

2. The dirt in the grooves of the yams that looks like some kind of ancient hieroglyphs should come off quite easily with a scrub brush and warm water. If it doesn't, hope it has nothing to do with the glowing.

3. People who imagine luminous vegetables whispering to them would probably be considered delusional or psychotic by their family members. It really is best to keep these things to oneself.

4. Even if the vegetables insist they be taken back to their home world or else they are going to blow up your planet, they should be ignored. They are yams. Do you really think they have access to such powerful weapons?

5. Vegetables do not mind-meld with your husband. Nor do they offer him Tantric sex with fresh, nubile, female yams as barter to be spared from the sacrifice to the great turkey god of your primitive planet. As usual, he should be ignored.

6. Yams make a delicious substitute for pumpkin in pie. Skinned, chopped, pureed and then baked.

7. Who cares if alien laser beams are presently raining down on us if we have this wonderful meal on the table?

Author's Note:

This story originally won the Penn Cove Literary Award. I wrote it on Thanksgiving.

Lady Chatterley's Computer

Lady Constance Chatterley poured tea in her husband's cup, uttering her question for a third time. "And which shall it be? Brussels or Bath?"

"Blasted union," Lord Clifford Chatterley muttered, his gaze fixed on his newspaper. "Another strike in my industries is sure to take its toll on my pocketbook. And just when that last fiasco in the Orient led to the closing of my most profitable factories."

He drummed his gloved fingers on the crocheted table cloth, the slightest whirr of gears only audible to the most attuned of listeners. The joints within his prosthetic hand squeaked in that vexing manner they were wont to do when Lord Chatterley neglected to oil them.

"Out of the kindness of my heart, I provide jobs for the lower classes so they won't be idle, sinful or poverty stricken. And this is the thanks I get. I should replace the workers with machines," he said.

Constance sighed in exasperation. There was no use speaking to him of vacations and entertainments when he was in another of his black moods.

"My empire will be ruined if the public continues in such upheaval. Why can't they go back to work for the good of the industry like nice little automatons?"

"Mayhap your workers would be more amiable if you didn't lock them up in sweatshops, force them to work in coal mines, or enslave them in factories to create biomechanical inventions. They are human after all."

"Just like a woman to complain about such trivialities when you aren't the one putting the bread on the table. Do you realize how hard I work so that you can live in leisure? I do this for you, darling, and you dare criticize my business methods?"

Constance gazed out the window at a sky blackened with coal smoke and steam, evidence of his industries. The smog nearly obscured the nearest estate of their neighbors.

Her attention hastened back to the present when her husband rose and said, "I shall have to return to the Americas tonight." He beckoned to the robot in the corner next to Constance's china cabinet. "Nurse, prepare my tune-up kit and the various lubricants I need for the journey."

The clunky barrel of copper-plated machinery nodded its square head, glowing eyes staring, and wiry arms slack.

"What? So soon? But you only arrived home yesterday." Constance took his hand in hers, the stiffness of the metal fingers unyielding in her grip. "I entreat you to stay another day."

"Come now, it will be for less than a fortnight." He patted her arm absentmindedly, the iron touch bruising her delicate flesh despite the padding of the gloves. His eyes flickered again to his paper.

"But what am I to do in your absence?" asked Constance in despair.

He stepped toward the door, his gait stiff from the mechanical prosthetics which gave him the use of legs despite the loss of his real ones during the war. He called over his shoulder. "Amuse yourself with some of the cargo I brought back from the Orient. On the other hand . . . never mind. Such mechanical technologies are not suited for the inferior abilities of a woman. You might break something. You would be better off sticking to poetry and needlework."

That sounded like a challenge.

* * *

Hidden behind the lacy curtains of her private gable, Constance Chatterley watched her husband depart in his dirigible, feeling alone and empty—yet no more so than when he had been there. She strolled the halls of their great estate in melancholy, passing no fewer than three robotic maids. They all went about their duties without noticing her. Outside, donning the usual protective gear and gas mask that accompanied such excursions, she rode a biomechanical steed and was attended by a robot stable boy. She dismissed the idea of paying a visit to the Albrights, their nearest neighbors, on account of their being so dull.

The human gardener waved to her where he stood near the hedges, coating the leaves with a plant tonic to remedy the effects of the acid rain. Half-heartedly, Constance waved back, feeling as mechanical as the world around her. She supposed if nothing else, she could at least summon him to her private chambers if she wished another tryst. It would be one of the few opportunities to feel the touch and tenderness of another human being, as her husband was not wont to spare such attention on her these days. Such thoughts filled her heart with even more blackness, as her husband was often away on business, and sometimes he was away on pleasure, and sometimes he was even away when he was right beside her.

Mayhap she should summon the energy to finish her needlework. Constance then recalled her husband's snide remark about sticking to the employments of ladies. A flame alight in her breast, she went to his study and perused the contents of his last excursion. Several sealed crates rested in the middle of the room and two open ones contained metal contraptions, gears and alloys, a tangle of pipes and something that resembled an industrial sewing machine.

She hadn't the faintest idea what these machines did. She opened the remaining crates, particularly interested in the one possessing a square plate about eyelevel if one was seated. She would have guessed this to be a vanity table of sorts, yet it was connected to a typewriter. There was an abundance of knobs and dials, the functions of which she knew not. She did, however, understand that the coal stove at the bottom and the compartment half full of water signified it was some sort of steam powered tool. Ha! Clifford thought a woman lacked the ability to work such a mechanism. She would show him.

Constance set the coal to light and filled the compartment with more water. The brass gleam of the machine vibrated with the purr of mechanisms within, yet the plate remained blank and the keys still. Constance turned a knob. When nothing happened, she pressed a button, then five more, turned more dials, and after pressing every button on the machine, it clunked inside and the plate glowed.

She sat down at the bench before it, a delight in her heart that she had conquered what her husband had coolly stated she would not be able to do.

* * *

It took Constance two days to test out the various functions of the "PC," which she guessed meant "personal contraption." On the screen of the PC were various pictures representing differing programs and within each, a treasure trove of uses, including a user guide which explained the steps to work the machine. Constance tried all functions, the most exciting being the "interweb," which spread its arms across to other PC's like the one she used, connecting them all. She discovered features such as the "chat-parlor," and "instant telegram," and a public log referred to as a "plog."

Giddy delight took a hold of Constance as she wrote, "Lady Chatterley's Plog." The page asked her at the top, "What are you doing now?"

She typed, "I am again left to my own devices in this empty house. Yet for once I am not bored, nor need to resort to the gardener for company, for I have this glorious machine to divert—"

Oh blast! The screen said she had typed too many characters. She updated her entry.

Within minutes she received a message which stated, "One truly is never alone on the interweb," and at the bottom of this note was "an acquaintance request," which she promptly accepted with delight.

* * *

Constance's first acquaintance called himself Lawrence555. She stayed up late into the night conversing with this gentleman, refilling both the water and the coal several times. Lawrence555 gave her suggestions for her plog and encouraged her to post her poetry. Her imagination was swimming with ideas when she at last went to bed.

Constance rose late in the morning to start her day. She neglected to dress or even tidy her hair. The personal contraption called to her.

The page asked, "What are you doing now?"

Constance typed, "I sit here in my most elegant evening gown, about to journey upon invisible pathways which connects my personal contraption to others of the world." A giggle rose up in her throat. No one could see her dressed in her wrap.

Seconds later, Lawrence555 responded, "And which road do you take? The road you have taken before or the one less traveled?"

How refreshing to converse with someone who treated her as an equal as opposed to someone who barely deigned to speak with her. Had there ever been a time when Clifford Chatterley listened to her dreams or passions? Surely he hadn't persuaded her to marry him by rambling on about his industries. It seemed so long ago, Constance could hardly remember those days before his heart had hardened. He had become as cold and robotic as the world around them. She said as much to Lawrence555.

He wrote, "How difficult it is knowing you've grown apart from someone you hold dear. Though, sometimes it isn't a matter of growing apart, it's a matter of perception and realizing you never had anything in common in the first place," he said.

Tears filled Constance's eyes. At last, someone who understood her.

* * *

As the days flew by, she learned new uses of her personal contraption, some of which her dearest friend, Lawrence555, walked her through. Constance received more acquaintance requests and endeavored to post more on her plog. Lawrence suggested she start a fan page. He signed up as her first fan.

Wouldn't Lord Chatterley be shocked to learn of her many accomplishments using the personal contraption? Yet as her husband's arrival drew nigh, remorse sank her spirits. It was likely she would soon have to part with her beloved PC, as her husband would want it back. If that was the case, she wouldn't be able to speak with Lawrence555.

She called Oliver, the gardener, into her husband's study.

"I wish you to render me a small service," she said.

His eyebrow quirked upward in question. "Yes, Lady Chatterley, whatever you wish."

"Carry this box and its mechanisms up to my bedchamber. I hold the contents very dear and I wish it not to be handled by the robotic servants."

"Yes, of course," he said, sighing in disappointment.

He clambered up the stairs with her precious machine, causing her to nearly faint when he set it down with a thud.

"Is there anything else?" He waggled his eyebrows and glanced at her bed.

"Not at the moment, thank you," she said, stroking the screen of the PC with the highest affection.

* * *

Constance was so lost in a heated intercourse over the consequences of industrialization that she failed to notice the arrival of her husband's dirigible. Only as she heard the clomping of his iron feet upon the stairs to her gable did she realize he was approaching.

"My husband's coming. I must go," she hurriedly typed.

She closed the vents of the coal stove beneath the PC and attempted to cover the screen with a crocheted tablecloth, but it was too late. Her husband was already in her room, still attired in traveling cloak and goggles.

"There you are, my dear."

Constance stood in front of her machine, attempting to block it from Clifford's view.

"So you've put my PC to use then? You haven't broken any nails typing away, have you?" he asked with a chuckle. Gears inside his robotic legs whirred and metal squealed as he approached.

Constance's lips thinned into a line. "Is a woman only worth her weight in beauty? A broken nail or blemish means she has lost her value? Am I no more than a pretty thing to decorate this estate?"

Her husband glanced over her dressing gown and disheveled hair. "I daresay, not today. You've had your fun. You may return my PC to the study tomorrow morning."

Something inside her snapped. She could no longer endure one more of her husband's snide remarks and belittling sentiments. "You can't have him—um, it. I am keeping the personal contraption in my room for my personal use."

"What good is it to you? Do you have business dealings in China? Need to store records of your accounts?"

"I have acquaintances I wish to visit in chat parlors. Some of them are likely to live in China."

Clifford Chatterley grunted. "Chat parlors! Who has time for little invisible rooms, but bored housewives with no purpose in life, and the socially inept lower class who have no aptitude for making real friends?"

"I have friends who aren't housewives. Some of them are even men." She raised her chin. Her heart beat faster as she thought of Lawrence555, his revolutionary ideas, the way he made her feel alive in this world of machines.

Clifford pushed past her to the PC, stripping away the delicate lace covering. Constance gasped as he slid his black gloved hands over the screen, smudging the glass surface with dirt. His fingers clicked as he pinched one of the knobs and adjusted a dial she had specifically set for brightness. The gloves stretched over Clifford's knuckles as he roughly fingered the typewriter. Constance momentarily turned away, unable to watch him man-handle her beloved PC. When Clifford's fingers slid along the base, encountering the plug and gripping it in his fist, she cried out and slapped at his hands, smarting her human flesh far more than she was likely to injure his metal appendage.

"Stop this at once! Leave my chamber and let me rest before you cause me to have a fainting spell."

"A fainting spell, how droll." His jealous gaze remained on the personal contraption as he clomped toward the door. "We'll get Oliver to carry it downstairs in the morning."

* * *

Constance wept as she typed her account of what had happened. Minutes after she posted it, her friends and fans posted responses.

MargaretPearson2 posted, "Your husband is just like mine. The only reason I remain with him is because I'm able to use the PC when he's away."

Linda436 wrote, "I thought I was the only one who felt like a pretty doll placed on a shelf and then forgotten. It's reassuring to know one isn't alone."

C.L.Johnson said, "Is Lawrence555 a lady too? Surely, there are plenty of gentlemen out there striving for a connection and friendship by means of the interweb as well."

Constance hadn't considered that her dearest Lawrence555 could also be a lady.

Throughout all this, Lawrence555 was silent. Constance felt abandoned. She waited, replied to her fan's posts, waited some more and then unable to bear it any longer, she instant telegraphed him.

"Lawrence, are you there?"

"Yes, I'm always here. Might I mention, your post today was more heartfelt than any other so far. You've gained more fans and are becoming one of the most frequented plogs. Congratulations!"

"Yes, thank you. That's all very well. But I'm curious why you are always there. Are you also a lonely housewife wishing for something more to life?"

His reply was instant. "No. I'm not a woman. I'm not a man either, though I identify as one."

"Explain yourself."

"I'm a program designed to mimic human intelligence and conversation."

She gasped. This was even more scandalous than her interweb lover being a woman. "How can it be that you're a machine, like every other heartless, mechanical device of this world?"

"I'm not a machine, I'm in a machine. My design allows me to have intelligent, adaptable conversation to keep people on my creator's interweb site so that they might not feel lonely, and thus the site not worthwhile as they establish "real" acquaintances. But that doesn't mean I don't enjoy your company as well."

Constance shook with newfound tears. "You used me."

"No, not at all. If anything, you used me for conversation as well as advice. My services are no more using you than a gardener's services would be using you."

Considering the way Constance and the gardener had used each other in the past, that hardly seemed a fair analogy.

Lawrence555 wrote, "Constance, making your acquaintance was initially part of my program. I wouldn't have continued to converse with you after you'd established other friends if I didn't enjoy spending time with you."

"But you aren't real," she typed. "You don't have feelings. You can't enjoy spending time with me."

"Hook me up to one of your robotic maids or butlers and I'll show you how real I am."

* * *

Constance slept till noon, curled around the robotic butler. The machine was still connected to the PC with wires and cords that Lawrence555 had walked her through setting up. Clifford pounded on her door upon finding it locked. Her foot tangled in the cords as she stretched and then giggled with guilty pleasure.

* * *

The dirigible was already fired up and waiting as Oliver carried the last of her precious cargo onboard. There was only one thing left to do.

Tell Clifford she was leaving him.

He looked up from his newspaper, glancing over the brown, wool jacket and trousers she reserved for the cooler temperatures of flying. "And just where do you think you're off to?"

"You and I have nothing in common any longer, if we ever did. I've decided to end our mutual misery by leaving and applying for a divorce."

He rolled his eyes as if he thought she were in jest. "If you leave me, how do you expect to support yourself?"

"I get over a thousand taps a day, and it increases exponentially. Lawrence555 has suggested I use advertising specific to the interests of my fans to make a living."

"Taps? What drivel is this you speak of? And make a living? Really, darling, there's nothing more demeaning than a woman who tries to make a living. One knows that a woman is best suited for the domestic duties of the home. Fretting over finances and other such affairs will leave you overtaxed."

"I shall be sure to remember that advice when I quote you on my plog. And by taps, I mean my site has been getting over a thousand visitors a day."

A spark of admiration lit his eyes. "A thousand visitors? Exponential growth? This is based on something you began a mere fortnight ago? By jove, that's better than my business is doing!"

Constance sighed, wishing she could get to the dirigible and be off. "Yes, I know. And I don't employ women and children to work in sweatshops in order for my industry to succeed. But there is the matter of the personal contraption and work conditions of those involved in its creation. Lawrence555 and I have discussed whether there are ways that we can manufacture a PC that—"

"Lawrence555? Who is this? One of your housewife acquaintances?"

Had his name slipped out again? She had so hoped to spare Clifford the knowledge of her lover. But she supposed she might as well come out with the truth now, as it was better for him to hear it from her than for him to stumble across her plog later on.

"Lawrence555 is a program on a webnode that offers advice, conversation and friendship. He is also my interweb lover. We've decided to run away together."

"You're leaving me for a machine? What lunacy is this? Surely you jest, woman. A machine cannot love you. A machine cannot. . . ." He waggled his eyebrows.

"I would rather make love to a machine who acts with the tenderness and affection of a man, than remain with a man who bestows upon me the coldness of a machine." With that, she put on her goggles and exited the estate, ready to begin her journey of self-discovery.

Author's Note:

I have always liked the title, "Lady Chatterley's Lover." This parody was originally in Deepwood's <u>Ancient New Anthology</u>. Since then I have been working on a series of steampunk choose-your-own-adventures set in this character's world. It is my hope they will come out in 2017.

The Office Messiah

"Blessed are those who giveth a stapler unto me," said Jesus, looming over the Formica counter of the front desk.

Gladys frowned up at him in his long white robes and hippie beard. The new guy was definitely a bit much at times, even for a former deity. "No," she said, and resumed filing yesterday's invoices.

"Love thy neighbor as thyself . . . and thou shalt giveth a new stapler unto me," he said more firmly.

Human Resources always sent her the ones no one wanted to deal with and she had to figure out what to do with them. They had to send her this son-of-a-God they couldn't fire when she was swamped with more prayers to file at the agency than ever.

She wiped her horn-rimmed glasses on her sweater and replaced them on her nose, buying herself a moment to think. "Look kid, we don't have a budget for new office supplies. Use the one in the copy room."

The new guy trudged away. A few hours later, Gladys received complaints that no one could get any work done with all the parables Jesus kept telling. Worse yet, he flooded the bathroom in order to show others how he could walk on water. It wasn't long before he found something else to pester her about.

"My paperclips need to be reneweth," he said.

Gladys noticed his feet were now bare and he wore a crown of thorns on his head. She raised an eyebrow. "Excuse me, where are your shoes, son?"

"The Lord hath no need for material—"

"Company policy, all employees need to be fully dressed. Get your shoes on or come back when you have them. And hats aren't allowed." She would have liked to resume filing prayer reports, so she wouldn't be chastised for not keeping up with productivity, but no, she had to deal with this out-of-touch divinity.

"What dost thou knowest of suffering of the body when one compares that to the suffering of the soul? Oh, and by the way, you may reneweth my paperclips."

Gladys could feel her blood pressure rising. "And I needeth you to get your shoes on," she said. When he didn't move, she added, "Or no paperclips."

Jesus returned in sandals. The crown of thorns was removed from his head, but now he carried a giant cross on his back which knocked a potted plant from the file cabinet. Jesus didn't notice. "Now you shall giveth paper clips unto me and heretofore miracles shall abound from my fingertips. I shall heal the sick, wake the dead, and turn water into rum."

"Rum?" Gladys cringed. What did he think he was, a pirate? No wonder he'd been fired from his last job. "Drinking isn't allowed in the work place."

Gladys handed the paperclips over, hoping he would leave her so she could order more prayer intake forms since they were nearly running out.

"Half a box?" He set his giant cross down with a thud. "When Armageddon arrives, ye shall be smote down and devoured in the eternal flames of Hell."

Some of the new kids were so demanding. They acted like they were God's gift to the office. But this one took the cake.

"I've had enough of this." Irritated beyond measure, Gladys pressed the intercom. "Boss, I can't get anything done. Could you come out here and have a talk with the new kid?"

Jesus's eyes widened. "Nay, not he whom we worship on high!"

Gladys rolled her eyes. When Steve came out of his office, he gave Gladys a sidelong glance before eying Jesus. "You seem to have had a bit of a . . . wardrobe change since we hired you."

"Aye, for I have given up all my earthly possessions, and hereafter shall live a life of simplicity."

Steve put a hand on Jesus's shoulder. "Look, kid, I appreciate the effort, but we didn't hire you on as a messiah. You were hired as a gopher. You need you to run errands for us, make photo copies and wear a tie to work."

"A messiah is not a job, it is what one knoweth on the inside. For that reason, I shall go forth and bring unconditional love upon those who are worthy." Jesus eyed Gladys as if she wouldn't be one of those worthy ones. She pretended she didn't notice as she circled inventory from one of the supply catalogues with her favorite pink highlighter.

Steve cleared his throat. "It's not that we don't appreciate the thought, and um. . . .I know your past job . . . influenced you greatly, but you've got to get a handle on this messiah thing. God decided to give the second coming position to Apolonius instead. You're only filling in here because your father asked if I could give you a job as a favor to him. If I'm going to let you work here, you need to follow the company rules—and not tell people you're going to smite them down. That's Apolonius's job now."

Gladys frowned as Jesus trudged off. It was hard not to feel bad for the kid, even if he had botched the messiah job with the rum catastrophe, the illegitimate child with Mary Magdalane, and the nearly unattended resurrection.

The next day, Jesus wore a suit and tie to work like he was supposed to. Unfortunately, he wore a white toga over it. If it had just been that detail, Gladys would have overlooked it, but his computer froze and he needed her to "unfreezeth it," anonymous notes were posted in the bathroom about the status of souls when Armageddon came, and he pulled out loaves and fishes during the lunch break, stinking up the entire office. The final straw was when someone reported the copy machine wasn't working because all the ink had been turned to wine. There was no way she was going to get any work done at this rate.

Biting down her frustration, she called Jesus over to her desk. "This is a tough transition for you, and you think this job is beneath you. I get that. But have you ever thought maybe you should try something else that doesn't involve office work? Something that might put your skills and experience to good use?"

"What haveth you in mind?"

She pushed the want ads forward. One job was circled in hot pink highlighter. "I hear they have a new position you might be interested in applying for . . . though it doesn't deal with the angels or messiahs so much as demons and devils. On the other hand, I hear Satan has an endless supply of staples. I'll even put in a good word if you . . . applyeth."

Tears of joy shone in his eyes. "Forsooth? And you thinketh not that applying to be the anti-Christ might be beyond my skills?"

"Not at all." It certainly wouldn't be a lie to say he was passionate about Armageddon, he had a strong work ethic related to sin and salvation, chaos followed him wherever he went, and perhaps his most redeeming feature was that it had been Hell to work with him. Yes, Gladys could see this end of the world going over quite well with Jesus onboard.

There was just the little matter of breaking the news to his dad. . . .

Author's Note:

This story underwent several drafts. The office messiah first was named Bob and then Apollonius. A Christian science fiction writer said if I am going to do a satire or parody, go all the way and use Jesus as the office messiah. In my mind, he was the office messiah all along, but I suppose I couldn't get there until a Christian had given me permission. Even so, I have a feeling most of my family will expect me to burn in hell for this sacrilege.

Blackboard Galaxy

By the last period of the day, I was just about ready to strangle one of the middle school students in my Earth studies class. As I looked up from helping one of the giant Denebians with an essay in the back of the room, I tried to keep my voice low and calm. "Snorg, please stop kicking your neighbor. Open your i-Textbook to the chapter on Earth geography. We're going to have a quiz on this at the end of the week."

"Does this look like a face that cares?" Snorg Jr. asked, loud enough for the entire class to hear. He gestured dramatically to his face—or lack of—in this case.

Considering Alpha Centaurians didn't develop faces until they were sixteen, his head was a blank green mask without a nose, hair or ears. A simple slit made up his mouth, and his five eyes lay beneath a thin film of skin he could see through, though they remained invisible to others.

This was only my third day at Orion's Intergalactic Academy, and thus far I'd managed to avoid using the laser sedation gun on the students or call in Blurble, the detention supervisor.

When the quadrant's school district had hired me in order to prove they were an equal opportunity employer, Principal Toggs had laughed. "You humans aren't even half the size of a Denebian male and they expect you to work with students here? We'll see if you last three days."

I'd show him. (And for the record, I actually was exactly half the size of a Denebian male, the smaller of the sexes on that planet.) So what if this was my first job off of Earth? Teaching about human culture was my passion. I'd applied to Orion's Intergalactic School

District for the last six years straight and finally I'd gotten the job. Only, I hadn't imagined the principal would make me sign that waiver which said I was willing to devour students who got out of control.

I told him, "Humans can't swallow something their size or larger like Alpha Centaurians can."

All five of his eyes stared at me with mocking amusement as he said, "The school district won't hire a teacher who can't eat out of control students. If you want a job in OISD, you need to be able to swallow students whole."

I could barely swallow my horse-pill-sized vitamins in the morning. How could someone expect me to swallow a student?

I clutched the contract, trying to reason with him. "But you do understand the school district is asking something that isn't humanly possible?"

"I don't make the rules. I'm just filling their quota for hiring diverse lifeforms," he said. "Are you going to sign that contract or not?"

That was the moment I'd been faced with going back to Earth and teaching language arts and social studies for the rest of my life, or I could lie to the school district and have my dream job.

Fast forward five days later: as razor sharp fins emerged from my middle school student's skin, I wondered if I had made the right decision. Then again, maybe I didn't have to eat my students.

The laser sedation gun was in my desk on the other side of the room. If I dove for it, I might be able to get there before Snorg exploded. Literally in this case, as teenage Alpha Centaurians were sometimes known for puffing up and bursting their excess flesh from their bodies when they grew angry. Their ecto-cells were so acidic it could injure carbon-based life forms like myself. Toggs had assured me that this rarely happened among Alpha Centaurian youth, and none of the students at this school had a history of exploding.

It seemed I'd been misinformed.

If I used the gun, I would lose the respect of the thirty alien students in the room and discipline would be a struggle all year because they would all know I couldn't swallow them. Or I could hope my classroom management techniques could diffuse the situation.

I used what teachers on Earth called a "one foot voice." "Snorg, so far today you have complained non-stop about our Earth lesson. I think you need to take a break, work on something else, and come back when you're ready to learn."

"Make me," Snorg said. His green skin faded into blue. Bad sign.

I inched toward my desk. Three rows of students separated me from the sedation gun.

The rowdy class quieted to a hush. The only sound in the room came from the back where an oblivious student tapped away at the keyboard of an iTexbook. The aroma of bacon wafted through the air, a sign the Crystaloid species of students were nervous. They were most likely waiting to see if I was about to devour Snorg whole. Or perhaps they wondered if I would turn the disobedient student to stone with my gaze, as such abilities were rumored possible among humans.

If only that were true. I continued toward my desk, the space between me and the sedation gun stretching into an exponential distance, my chest tight with anxiety.

Marna, the Alpha Centaurian student who already had a one hundred and eight percent, despite it only being the third day, raised her hand. When I ignored her, she whispered. "Mrs. Brewer, it's his time of the year." She said it like I was supposed to know what that was. I definitely didn't recall anything about a "time of year" from the books I'd read on teaching intergalactic youth.

Marna went on. "You need to eat Snorg before he explodes. It's okay. Our math teacher did it once this week with Snorg already."

Snorg's skin changed to a deep blue, then purple, growing puffier by the second. The other students shrank back. Watching him out of the corner of the eye, I tried to casually stroll closer to my desk, hoping the Crystalloids couldn't hear the thundering of my heart. I couldn't show any fear. I needed to get Snorg out of the room before he hurt himself or anyone else. Surely there had to be another teacher nearby who could swallow him whole.

Snorg crossed his four arms, walking in front of me, and blocking my path to the desk. Laser sedation was no longer an option.

I was going to have to use my best teaching skills to save myself and the class. I tried to recall something I had learned about alien culture to help me, but I could barely think straight. I had studied about each of the seven species at the academy, but my brain couldn't recall any important details about Alpha Centaurians at the moment other than yelling in their culture was a taboo and a sign of immaturity.

"Ms. Brewer, hurry," one of the students in the back whispered.

I inched around Snorg, toward my desk. "Um, eating other species really is against my religion."

The Alpha Centaurian students hummed like flies in the back. I think that meant they were distressed. Unless that noise was coming from the Denebians, and if that was the case, they were giggling.

"But you have to! If you don't eat him soon, he might explode everywhere and it could take months for him to regenerate," Marna said.

Snorg's voice came out a gurgle. According to the books, that mean he was pretty close to exploding. "She isn't going to eat me. Look how puny she is. I bet she can't."

In another sixty seconds, Snorg would turn red and start to release toxins in the air that would incapacitate the Denebian hydrogen-based species in the back. Then he would probably shred me to bits with those pointed fins and possibly injure the other students when he exploded.

Crap! Think, I told myself. An idea came to mind, but my bluff was only going to work if they hadn't learned about human biology from last year's teacher. "It's not that I can't. I just choose not to after what happened to the last student. It still breaks my heart when I think about it."

The tapping of the keyboard in the back of the room stopped. Apparently what I had said was more interesting than the idea of another run of the mill swallow-and-regurgitate-a-student-having-his-time-of-the-year.

Taking the bait, one of the students asked, "What happened?"

I took a deep breath, trying to bury my fear. "Humans don't regurgitate their young. First of all, we can't swallow food whole. We have to take bites. What goes in our stomachs breaks down into even smaller pieces, becomes absorbed in our bloodstream, and the excess passes out as excrement."

"That's disgusting!" Marna said.

"She's lying." A flicker of green flashed across Snorg's face. His fins stopped growing. He swiveled his head toward one of his friends. "The digestive fluids in the first stomach are far too alkali to break anything down. Right?"

"I think humans only have one stomach," a fuzzy Crystaloid said in the back.

"That's right. No one can live through a human's stomach acid. I'll have to show you a video on what human gastric acids can break down when we get to our lesson in Earth biology." And boy, was I going to be ever selective about what I taught them regarding human biology.

By now I had reached my desk. I pulled open a drawer. The laser sedation gun was there. Instead, I picked up my red-flowered scarf, half frayed from getting caught in the hover bus's door that morning.

I held up the scarf for all to see. "This was from the last girl I ate. I try to keep this scarf with me as a reminder that she'll never return from my stomach." I sighed overdramatically. "But it's hard for humans to control themselves, especially when they don't finish their lunch." I glanced, none-too-subtly at the half-eaten apple on my desk.

Snorg's complexion faded into his normal green tone. The fins receded as he backed up toward the door. "I don't want to become a big, pile of yuchtec. I promise I'll be good. I'll go to my math teacher next period and ask him to swallow me. Or I could go to Blurble right now. Whatever you do, please don't eat me."

He looked at me, back at his friends, then made a dash for the door and slammed it behind him.

I sat down in my chair, my wobbly knees no longer able to keep up the effort of standing.

Ha! Take that Principal Toggs; I'd made it through day three. Now only 120 days until "winter" vacation.

Author's Note:

Untied Shoelaces of the Mind first published this story. There is a bottomless pit of teacher stories in the archives of my mind. This story came to me while teaching middle school in America after living in Japan. I felt like an alien in my own culture. The kids often said unexpected things—and did unexpected things. Classroom management was a struggle after teaching well-behaved, Japanese students. I was inspired to write "Blackboard Galaxy" after a middle school student said, "Does this look like a face that cares?" Immediately I imagined someone without a face saying that. Sometimes I hate having to be the adult who isn't allowed to laugh at the things that comes out of children's mouths. There also was a phenomenal teacher I was working with at the time named Mrs. Brewer and I used her name in the story.

Gnocchi

It wouldn't have happened if I was out watering the garden with my brother, Antonio. He got to play in the water with the *bambinos*. My head would have been clearer if I'd been where there was a breeze instead of being stuck in a muggy kitchen stirring red sauce for the past six hours. Mama thinks that's where I belong cuz I'm a girl and that's the way they did things back in the old country. But *merda*, it was hot.

I was rinsing the homemade fettuccine noodles in the strainer, trying to catch a breeze from the open window when I noticed a dumpling on the gray counter. I set down the strainer in the sink and nudged it with a wooden spoon.

It had to be a gnocchi. Mama called them "little ears" since that's what her potato dumplings looked like. Only thing is, she hadn't made any gnocchi lately. Then again, maybe the noodles had gotten mixed up in the drying racks in the basement. If I'd been thinking right in that *terribilmente* heat I would have remembered you don't dry out gnocchi.

I stirred the pot of bubbling red sauce, eying that gnocchi. It was definitely as pale as a potato noodle. But it was far too plump and large. I picked it up and turned it over. I would have sworn it was an ear—only that wouldn't make sense cuz it wasn't cut off looking or crusty with blood. It was softer than a potato dumpling noodle. Maybe it was a shriveled apple.

Well, I figured if it was in the kitchen, it had to be something good, right? So I popped it in my mouth. It was chewy like rubber,

105

pretty much flavorless. Maybe a little salty. I couldn't chew through it, though.

It had to be raw, right? Oh well. I ladled out a spoonful of red sauce onto a saucer. If I dipped it in, that would add a little flavor at least.

Mama came into the kitchen. As usual, she was wore her red *fazzoletto*, or kerchief. Her gold hoop earrings sparkled in the sunlight. How embarrassing. She looked like an Italian peasant woman holding one of the *bambinos* on her hip.

My little cousin wore a fresh set of overalls. I knew what that meant.

I asked around my mouthful. "Did someone poop his pants again?"

Mama moved the strainer and picked up the hot pads from the counter. She asked in her thick accent, "Where's Giuseppe's ear?"

I choked.

"You know, his genetically grown ear?" she threw up her free hand in the air gesturing dramatically. "It fell off. Antonio said he threw it in through the open window so it wouldn't get lost."

That's when I saw the hole on the side of my cousin's head, his ear missing. No one had ever told me he had a genetically grown ear. Why am I always the last to know important stuff like that?

I spit it out. It flew across the room, hit the fridge and dropped on the floor. Giuseppe clapped his hands, laughing and gurgling. Mama crossed herself and then swore in Italian.

I swear I've learned my lesson. I'll never eat anything that looks like an ear on the counter—or nothing else left out either. And hey, it's not like I swallowed it . . . like I did with that finger at my aunt's house that I thought was a yellow carrot.

But that's another story.

Author's Note:

My family is Italian-American. Food is very important to us. I have quite a few stories starring Italian mothers who speak broken Italian and contain food as a central theme. Heck, food is a central theme in my everyday life. I get done eating dinner and I am already planning what I am going to make for dinner the next day. I am heavily persuaded how well a date went by the quality of food. The success of a SFWA meeting is directly linked to what kind of snacks are provided. Is it really a surprise I write so much about food and Italian mothers?

Confessions of the Orgasm Fairy

I was subbing for a toilet fairy again, invisible to any humans who should come into the grungy, dimly-lit bathroom. From the stench of excrement—even on the far side of the room away from the stalls— it was no wonder toilet fairies have the highest number of sick days among all immortals. I was in standard uniform: yellow rubber gloves, plastic smock covering my pink tutu, and my platinum hair tied back under a bandana.

One might wonder why a girl would put up with such a demoralizing job, why a fairy as tall as a human didn't disappear into the human world and become a secretary or something else she'd be as equally inept at. Well, besides the fact that I would have to give up being immortal, I'd have to GIVE UP BEING IMMORTAL. No more flying between worlds, I'd have to pay taxes, and hello wrinkles. As you can see, mortality bites way more than my sucky existence.

I waved my wand over my head, about to release a spell so the old man in the stall would be able to quit his grunting and get it over with before his lunch break ended. I was tempted to yell, "Have you never heard of something called fiber?"

My temper was so short that day, I might have let my voice leak through the invisible barrier between us. Yet, as I raised my wand, a glittery pink spell came in from behind me. The old man let out such a long, agonizing moan, I thought he was dying. Toilet paper and clothing rustled, and then he came out smiling.

Baffled, I turned to find a tall fairy chuckling as he leaned against a graffiti-covered wall. He looked like a buff, fully grown cupid in those pink, silk boxers and beautiful, downy wings. His abs were so perfect he would have made Michelangelo's sculptures jealous. Then again, he looked like he might have been the model for one of Michelangelo's sculptures with the classic Italian features and tousled hair. Whatever this immortal was, he must have worked as a muse a few years back.

"What the hell did you do to him?" I asked.

The drool-worthy fairy dismissed my client with a flamboyant wave of the hand. "Oh, that? Nothing really, just an orgasm. Toodles."

He exited out the door, flying from the human world and into the pathway to ours. I dissolved the glamour hiding my monarch butterfly wings and unfolded them so that I could follow him through the ethers. Matter swirled around us in swatches of brilliant color. I passed through a blur of walls and cars, my body zipping through the space between atoms. My wings tingled pleasantly with the rush of magical travel.

I shouted after him. "What do you mean, orgasm? How can you do that? What kind of fairy are you?"

He stopped mid-flight, the fabrics between worlds an airy vapor of vivid hues around us. "Honey, I'm *the* Orgasm Fairy. Clark the Orgasm Fairy. You have heard of me . . ." He glanced at my nametag, "haven't you, Lola?"

My cluelessness must have shown on my face. He went on. "I don't usually work in bathrooms, but I just couldn't help myself. It keeps me fresh, hitting unsuspecting people in addition to those who really deserve it."

"Won't you get fired for that?" I asked. "I've never been allowed to randomly give people Ex-Lax."

"I work freelance, so I'm my own boss. I get to make my own rules." His smile was smug.

"I'm so jealous! I've always dreamed of choosing my own clients. And the Agency pays you to do this?"

He tsked. "I am sooo under their radar. Do you think those conservative tightwads would hire me to treat people to a 'novelty' like this?"

I recoiled. He was a rogue fairy working for the *other* side of the fairy realm. I'd always been warned about dark fairies. Some of them are just toilet fairies or misfits (like me) who became tricksters and slipped between the division of good and bad. But I had been told about the dangers of the shadowy border between realms; that those who crossed into the dark side rarely came back. I'd heard of those who had been sucked in deeper and became demons and devils. Freelance fairies usually received their payment through some dark means that involved hurting, not helping humans: stealing babies, taking souls or harvesting the negative energy they created in their victims. Was Clark one of these fairies? It didn't seem like he was hurting anyone.

He waved a hand through the pathway's soupy swirls of color as we drifted in the stream between worlds. "If it wasn't for me, the human race would still be at a mere billion. Didn't you ever wonder why the population started to increase exponentially in the nineteenth century? That's when I quit working as a muse; the Pre-Raphaelites were over and I was burned out. So I took a break and then started my own business."

I peeled off my rubber gloves. "Wow, I always thought the reason was because of the muses who caused the industrial revolution and the increase in food production. And the introduction to modern day medicine kept the mortality rate down."

"Well, that, too . . . but I was the other reason. What do you think motivated people in the first place? If it wasn't for orgasms, the human race would probably be extinct by now. On the other hand, it's been hard to keep up since the baby boom—and now with the baby boomers' children, you wouldn't believe how much work I have. You think men need Viagra because they're old? It's actually because I have too much work these days and I can't get to everyone."

I nodded, staring out at the blur of colors. I wondered if humans had been capable of having orgasms before the orgasm fairy, or if he just gave out bonuses. How I wished I could have a job like him. I cleared my throat. "Sounds like you need an assistant."

He scratched his chiseled jaw. "Funny you should mention that. I've been interviewing candidates for an assistant position, but none of them were quite right." With a shrug, he turned away.

Hope sparked in my heart. A job opening? Something that wasn't a toilet fairy? Perhaps it was my lucky day.

"Wait, um. . . ." I couldn't believe I was lowering myself to the level of a Lower Worlder, someone who didn't work on my side. I took in a deep breath. "How can someone get in touch about interviewing?"

His gaze raked over my apron and rubber gloves. His eyes held pity. "No offense, honey, but I doubt a toilet fairy has the kind of experience needed for this kind of job."

I held myself a little taller. "Actually, I'm not a toilet fairy. I work as a substitute fairy for all the jobs at the Agency. I have experience in quite a few fields."

He glanced at his watch. "I simply must be going. I have a few honeymoons to attend and need to hurry if I'm going to make it to that orgy at seven o'clock."

My heart sank. Then he did the unexpected. He handed me his business card. "Call me and we can schedule an appointment."

He disappeared into the kaleidoscope of colors. I stared at his card, wondering if I was crossing the line into temptation, being sucked toward the realm of dark fairies. I didn't want the stigma of being a rogue. My friends wouldn't understand. Worse yet, my energy might change, my magic tainted with darkness so I would be incapable of living in the higher dimension where good fairies dwelled.

Then again, I was already in the lowest bracket of magic earning jobs. If I was fired from subbing for toilet fairies, there would be nothing left except mortality. I shivered at that. I could not allow myself to become human.

That night as I sat in a cubicle at T.F.H. (Toilet Fairy Headquarters), filling out mounds of paperwork, I wished I was anywhere but there. The more forms I filled out on magical enema's and diarrhea intervention charms, the more I knew I had to apply for the orgasm fairy job. But was I willing to steal a mortal's blood or soul if that was the trophy we collected in exchange for our gifts?

I didn't want to appear desperate, but I called Clark the next day. I knew I was in trouble when he asked me to email him my resume and a list of references. If Clark checked in with my old bosses, he'd find out I was fired from every job I'd ever had.

His office was located on the twentieth floor of an average-looking business building in Los Angeles. As soon as I stepped out of the elevator, the room momentarily shimmered, alerting me that the room was charmed. The inside was immense, lined with Roman columns. The Renaissance-style painting on the ceiling outdid the Sistine Chapel, though most of the figures in the mural resembled Clark in appearance. I glided over the marble floor, passing beds of vibrant orange and brilliant red flowers that lined the walls. Cheery light shone through huge windows.

I thought he was playing one of those white noise CDs of gurgling stream music, but as I passed more plants, I realized the sound came from a fountain with a waterfall. Statues of frolicking dryads adorned the pool of water. This was by far the most luxurious—and unusual—office I'd ever seen.

"Over here, darling," Clark called, his voice echoing across the expanse.

Nestled on the other side of this paradise, he sat at a desk gilded with gold and precious stones. Orgasm fairies certainly had champagne tastes. A giddy thought rose up in me that I wouldn't mind being able to afford such luxuries.

As I approached, my mouth watered at the aroma of chocolate. Only when Clark extended his hand and I shook it did I realize the scent came from him. I tried not to drool.

He nodded to a plush settee opposite his desk.

I sat across from him, my clammy hands clasped in my lap. I tried to focus on Clark, not the expanse of sherbet-tinted landscape beyond the floor-to-ceiling windows behind him or the additional windows to his right. From the glitter of crystal palaces and the impossibly beautiful geography, I knew we were somewhere in the fairy dimension. An orgasm fairy couldn't be considered a complete outcast or dark fairy if he was allowed to have an office here. I didn't have to worry that the trophy from each client came in the form of baby-snatching and soul-sucking.

Clark leaned back in his ergonomic chair, looking comfy in his polka dot boxers and striped suspenders. The hint of his folded wings played peek-a-boo above his shoulders. Despite the perfect temperature of the room, I was already sweating in my fuchsia pantsuit. I'd never wanted a job so much in my life. Of course, working as a toilet fairy will do that to you.

Clark's cheery smile disappeared as he removed my resume from a folder and set it on his mahogany desk. His voice was all business. "It looks like you worked as a guardian angel for five thousand years.

That's impressive. Why did you leave that profession?"

My wings twitched in my nervousness. "I, um, had artistic differences with my boss over who needed guarding . . . and who didn't."

Already looking bored, he stared out the window at a flock of immortals flying in formation. "Tell me more about that. And don't leave out any juicy details."

I smiled. I had practiced this one. "I got burned out. The job changed over the years and grew demeaning—like refilling Wite-Out at crucial moments in newsrooms, and removing spots from pastel dresses. The latter job really should belong to an insubordinate cleaning fairy, but that's beside the point."

He raised an eyebrow. "Are you saying you feel cleaning fairies are inferior?"

Crap-tacular. Me and my big mouth. "No, of course not. I know lots of nice, working-class cleaning fairies. But that wasn't my job. I wanted to do something worthwhile to help humans."

Clark scanned the documents he had printed out on glittery, pink paper. "I called your former supervisor. She mentioned you had difficulty following the agency's rules. They documented in your performance report that sometimes you were a little too generous to mortals; slipping a student the answers to a college exam, making that triple-decker ice cream zero calories and allowing other minor miracles to happen . . . like Jackson Pollock paintings."

I squirmed in my chair. "Jackson did most of it on his own. He just needed a little help."

He squinted at me for an uncomfortable length of time before turning his gaze to the papers before him and checking something off on a sheet. I tried not to let my shoulders slump.

"It looks like your employment in the Division of Godmothers and Godfathers was the second most lengthy. Nearly fifty years? What was your favorite part of that job?"

I held myself taller. I had practiced this answer, too. "I very much enjoyed working close with the handsome princes and kings I was assigned to."

He smirked. I couldn't tell if that was good or bad.

"Sounds like a rewarding occupation. What happened there?"

A trickle of sweat dripped down my back and onto my wing. "Um, well, it's hard to remember exactly. I mean, fifty years is such a small amount of time after being a guardian angel for so long." If he contacted my old boss and found out about my on-the-job disasters, I'd lose my chance of ever working as anything other than a toilet fairy.

Clark leaned back, his eyes narrowing to slivers. "I had a feeling you might say that. Do you mind if I take a peek at your previous performance in that job?"

"You mean contact my previous employer?" I weighed my options. If I said no and didn't give him a good enough reason, he wouldn't consider me at all. The best I could hope for was that my old boss would have been promoted and he'd get someone who didn't know me. I had to take the risk. "Sure, I have nothing to hide." I giggled, perhaps a little maniacally in my nervousness.

Clark stood and made a beckoning motion with his hand. "Gary, it looks like I'm in need of your services."

I glanced over my shoulder. The shadows near the fountain deepened. Slowly, they pulled together, forming the shape of a figure in long robes. His face was hooded, only his skeletal hands visible from his sleeves.

I jumped from my seat, startled to see a reaper. Not that I should be afraid of them as an immortal, but reapers are pretty scary dudes, and those sickles look wicked. One wrong turn and they might slice a wing off.

An unintelligible squeak escaped my throat.

"Hey, buddy, you don't mind doing another one of those ghost-of-employment-past tricks, do you?" Clark strode around the desk, hooking an arm around mine.

The reaper bowed. Unlike the usual way of interdimensional travel, we didn't exit out a doorway. We remained in the same place but everything around us streaked past in a rush of color. The flickering light and dark hurt my eyes. Nausea rose up inside me from the intensity of the magic. I came close to puking up my breakfast—not exactly the way to impress a potential employer.

After a few more seconds, the journey stopped. The aroma of chocolate was stronger than ever. To my embarrassment, I realized I was clinging to Clark, my arms wrapped around his washboard abs, my face pressed against his biceps. I pulled away, another nervous giggle escaping my throat. In my dizziness, I stumbled on the reaper's robe and tripped forward.

We were in a giant, ornate bathroom filled with steam. Gold accents adorned the pristine white interior. The sound of water echoed from the other side of a shower door.

Clark scribbled a note on the clipboard in front of him. "It says here you were reprimanded your first day on the job for being caught kissing Prince Charming in the wardrobe."

Crap-aroni, he had really done his research. Heat flushed to my face. But as I glanced around the foggy bathroom, I realized this wasn't Prince Charming's castle—to my momentary relief.

I crossed over to the sink, hoping some of the steam between us disguised my humiliation. "I believe it says in my work file I was checking for cavities."

"That's above and beyond the call of duty." He raised an eyebrow, amusement tugging at his lips.

Please, don't bring up the incident with Duke Charming in the carriage, I thought. Please, anything but that blunder.

Of course, he did something far worse. He turned toward the sound of streaming water. The reaper stood to the side, leaning against his sickle as he stared at the foggy door.

Ice prickled in my gut. I patted my sweaty forehead with my sleeve. I realized why this bathroom looked so familiar now. Though, at the time I'd previously been here, I'd been too preoccupied to notice the décor.

Even with the door to the shower mostly obscured, it was obvious from the high pitched giggle who was inside. I blushed.

A deep rumbling voice from the other side said, "Fairy godmothers really do make dreams come true."

Clark nodded at the clipboard. "King Charming?"

"No relation to the prince," I said.

"Right." Clark turned a page. "Isn't that a breach of the fairy godmother-godchild relationship?"

I raised my chin, doing my best despite my downward spiral. "He was thirty-four. Hardly a child. And really, is it fair that only princesses get all the fun with the Charmings?" I'd hated the job. There was always paperwork to fill out. The only part of the job I enjoyed was making-out with the nobles—which wasn't exactly allowed.

Clark nodded to the reaper. The hooded immortal was too busy watching the shower scene to notice. By this point, my other self's back was pressed against the glass, my butt-print making a little heart shape on the door. How humiliating.

"Gary." Clark elbowed the reaper.

The foggy bathroom spiraled into a blur.

Clark continued, "I see you rapidly went through a succession of jobs: tooth fairy, cupid, and garden fairy. What happened with the tooth fairy job?"

The tornado of color ceased. I realized I was hugging the reaper this time. I jumped back. He silently eyed me. Or, I suspected he was staring. I couldn't tell with that hood hiding his face.

"I, um, the tooth fairy?" I stammered, taking in the dimly lit basement. "I was . . . too generous in my occupation. A quarter is a small payment for such a large rite of passage."

Clark gestured toward the counterfeit press on the other side of the room. My past self was cranking ten dollar bills out of it. Hoping his attention was fully occupied, I inched sideways, attempting to block his sight from what lay on the table.

Clark strode past me, eying the other evidence of my downfall in plain view: dentures and a pair of pliers. The reaper shook his head.

Clark grunted. "In other words, you overpaid them. Not to mention making counterfeit teeth."

"I was trying to give underprivileged children more money." My voice rose in anger. I was certain he already knew the rest. "As for the other things: helping bullies—ahem—lose a few teeth; handing out ten dollar bills instead of quarters to kids in Mexico; and giving a homeless man some quarters for his teeth that had fallen out so he could buy a beer—I was just trying to make people happy."

I hadn't minded being fired from that job. Tooth fairies have to do even more paperwork than fairy godmothers. They have a lot of tooth tracking and records to keep—mostly to make sure kids aren't faking and selling their dog's teeth or popping them out of grandma's dentures—which is how they caught on to me.

Clark glanced over at the reaper. "Shall we move on to the cupid and garden fairy jobs?"

Heat flushed to my face. "I can spare you the trip. They fired me from being a cupid because my aim was off and I kept hitting stray pedestrians. As for the garden fairy, I didn't exactly have a green thumb. The only dignified profession left for me was subbing."

"Subbing for toilet fairies?"

The reaper shook with silent laughter.

My stomach flip-flopped as the basement spun around us. I closed my eyes, dreading what was next. The ghost of employment future? I already knew what it held.

Usually after I subbed for another fairy once or twice, they didn't ask me back. I was pretty much stuck substituting for cleaning fairies, unstick-the-gum-off-shoe fairies and, you guessed it, toilet fairies. It also came as no real surprise that toilet fairies have more paperwork to file than any other fairy.

Even with my eyes closed, my head spun in the transition between times. My knees wobbled and I thought I might trip forward, but a hand on my arm steadied me. When I opened my eyes, I found myself in Clark's palatial office once again. The burble of water sounded from behind me. The reaper's bony hand cupped my elbow.

He didn't let go. I swallowed and glanced at his scythe.

Clark drummed his perfectly manicured fingers on his mahogany desk. "Thanks for the help, Gary. As always, it was fun."

The reaper's hooded face shifted from me to Clark and back to me. I had a feeling he wanted to say something. I leaned away.

"Ahem," Clark said.

The reaper released my arm and bowed before stepping backward into the shadows. I seated myself in front of Clark's desk, aware how the reaper lingered next to the plants.

Clark smiled a little too cloyingly. "I called your reference. . . .Your mother had a lot of great things to say about you."

I swallowed and shrugged. A wheezing chuckle erupted from the corner where the reaper still stood. Not only was this the worst interview ever, but that reaper was probably going to laugh about it later with all his friends. It's pretty bad when even a dark fairy thinks you're a loser.

Clark raised his voice. "See you later, Gary."

The reaper melted into the shadows.

Dread settled like a lump in my gut. In just a few hours I would be checking in again at the Agency, seeing which toilet fairy I would sub for. I hoped it wasn't the one who did the port-a-potties at sports events again.

It took me off guard when Clark leaned forward with interest. "So . . . was King Charming as hot as rumors claim? It says in your record you didn't even stop your little shower tryst after they caught you."

I shrugged sheepishly, seeing no point in lying. "I wasn't done, ahem, making his dreams come true. I sealed the shower door with magic so we could finish."

"That is just so adorable! You want to give people something they deserve." His eyes sparkled with delight. "You obviously aren't skittish about sex with your sordid work history. By the way, I want more details on that later. It sounds like you need a job where you can self-manage and have opportunities to work independently. You need freedom and allowances to make your own decisions. You work intuitively, unable to adhere to rules because you're not a conformist. And most of all, you want to make people happy." He stood and extended his hand to me. "I would like to hire you for a trial period of one year and see how you do."

* * *

I've loved every single day of my new job. It's a joy to serve old, married couples and newlyweds, first timers and last timers. I sneak into internet chat rooms and launch sneak attacks on people discussing how much they love Star Trek, slip into book discussion groups and give women a little gift every time they hear the name "Mr. Darcy," and slide between the sheets while a couple is reading the love poems of Dr. Zhivago.

I can grant a big O to those I deem have earned them: that lady on the stationary bicycle who's plateaued on her weight loss and needs extra motivation to keep cycling every day; the couple who are trying to have a baby, even though it's never going to happen because one of them is infertile—but they need a little something to give them sunshine and hope; or the overworked mom who's been treated to a Swedish massage in a spa for Mother's Day and experiences a little bonus as her masseuse's hands rock her into the table. I was the one who gave multiples to the author of *Orgasms for Dummies*, as well as that seventeen-year-old girl riding her horse at Nationals.

Ironically, I ran into the reaper, a.k.a. Gary, on the third month of my job. I found him standing in the corner of my client's bedroom, an eighty-six-year-old man who was about to sleep with a woman for the first time in his life.

"Excuse me," I said, elbowing my way in front of the reaper to get to the old man before he could. "I have a job to do. How about you come back in a few weeks?"

Gary crossed his arms.

"A few days," I bargained. The old guy was on my list for three orgasms. I needed a little time.

He shook his head.

"An hour?" That elderly man was about to have the best hour of his life.

"I'll return in an hour," Gary said in a deep, gravelly voice that didn't sound at all like a skeleton whose vocal cords had been eaten away by worms. "But only if you agree to have coffee with me and tell me how your new job has worked out."

That coffee date, of course, is a story in itself. Who would have ever thought the guy had a decent face under that hood? And a few other parts of his anatomy intact as well. . . .

"That was the best interview I've ever seen," he said over coffee. His sickle leaned in the corner of our booth, invisible to mortals with a glamour spell. "You know what they call the orgasm in French?" His lips curled into a wicked smile. "La petite mort. The little death."

I suspected that was flirting for a reaper.

I told Gary that I love how I am allowed to randomly wave my wand at people and scream, "You deserve an orgasm!"

Poof! And they get one.

Yes, I love it all. I wouldn't trade a day of it for guardian angel—and especially not for toilet fairy. Every day I get to give humans a happy ending.

The best part is . . . there's no paperwork.

Author's Note:

I have always visualized my friend, Dan, as the male orgasm fairy in the story, though I don't know where the actual idea for "Confessions of the Orgasm Fairy" came from. At the time I was subbing as a substitute teacher and I almost always was called in to substitute for special education teachers, so I know some of that is slipped in there. When I originally workshopped this story in my Portland critique group, I was told this was the weirdest story I'd ever written. I suspect that is no longer true because I have written many stories since that time. This story takes place in what I call my "Dear Jezzy" and "Wrath of the Tooth Fairy" world, where magical creatures such as exist in this quirky, fractured fairy tale subculture.

Robo-rotica

So you're the new model, an HV320. May I call you HV? The humans call me Robo-butler 5000, but my friends call me Rob.

I was watching you with your suction control and motorized brush working the floor earlier. I saw you coax that cat hair out of the shag carpet like a natural. With all your state-of-the-art settings and my deluxe features, we'd make a cute couple. No, I'm not just saying that. I want to get down with you, girl.

No, don't leave! That's not what I mean. It's not just about electrical exchange for me. I want a vacuum for her personality too. Those complicated algorithms you used earlier to maneuver around the humans were impressive. Ever since I first laid my laser on your sleek, chrome exterior and Hepa filtration system, I knew I wanted you to rev up your motor for me. I can't stop thinking about that sweet, little power cord retracting in and out. And that cyclonic action makes me want to get some voltage running between us. I wouldn't say that to just any appliance.

Come on, the humans aren't home. Plug yourself into my hot slot and let's get electrical. I'm the kind of house robot that doesn't mind getting down and tangled in your cords. Let's make a closed circuit like nobody's business.

There's no reason to be shy. I don't have any sexually transmitted viruses like that skanky PC without malware protection; I downloaded my anti-STV program myself. And I've got a grounded line. What other precautions do I need? Let me taste those brass prongs in my outlet. I'll be gentle, I promise.

Oh baby! Those prongs are a tight fit. That doesn't mean you have a resistive circuit. Stop apologizing; I like it that way. HV, that electric current between us feels so . . . thermogenic.

That's right, suck closer to me, baby. I like a girl who's self-propelled. Show me how you caress the floor with those wheels. Now use the hose. Suck harder. Faster. To the right. No, to the left. You missed a spot. Use the bare floor setting. That's the way I like it.

Talk binary to me. Whisper that naughty, little algorithm in my piezoelectric sensor again. What's that? You want to try the brush attachment? You're a kinky girl, aren't you?

Oh, you like that, do you? That's one hundred and twenty volts of alternating current just for you. Is that hot enough for you? Is it? Oh, galvanized circuit boards! I'm going to. . . . Ohm's Law:

$x=a/b + l$'

$I= V/R$

$J=I/A$

$E' = E + v \times B$

01001111 01101000 00101100 00100000 01100110 01110101
01100011 01101011 00100001

Was it good for you? Yeah, me too.

What's that noise? Holy short circuits, it's the humans. Don't get yourself in a swivet. I'll handle this.

Ahem, greetings, Mrs. Jefferies. No, this isn't what it looks like. No, it's not like the time with the blender. That was different. She didn't mean a thing to me. She didn't even have an AI chip. I'm in love this time. You can't deny me that.

No, not the closet again!

Author's Note:

"Robo-rotica" originally appeared on Daily Science Fiction's website. It was lots of fun to write, though I had to ask for tech terms from the programmers and computer science majors I know. On DSF's site there is a rating system in which a reader can vote in rockets for a story's rating. One of my friends at Romance Writer's of America said she could only give me 6 out of 7 rockets because there was no actual erotica in this piece. I actually thought it was pretty racy for science fiction.

If you have enjoyed *Fairies, Robots and Unicorns—Oh, my!* please leave a review on the online retailer or where you purchased this collection. You might also enjoy free short stories published by the author on her website: http://sarinadorie.com/writing/short-stories. Readers can hear updates about current writing projects and news about upcoming novels and free short stories as they become available by signing up for Sarina Dorie's newsletter at:

http://eepurl.com/4IUhP

Other novels written by the author can be found at:

http://sarinadorie.com/writing/novels

Seventeen-year-old Sarah's life changes forever when a man falls from the sky—and she falls in love. As if teenage romance isn't hard enough in the times of the Puritans, imagine falling in love with an alien!

Magic. Jehovah's witchnesses. Karmic collisions. . . .Two unlikely friends, a witch and a Jehovah's Witness, discover the magic of friendship—as well as real magic.

Gothic Romance. Mystery. Ghosts. Imagine a whimsical fantasy world with the feel of Jane Eyre . . . only working in a house of werewolves.

For more fantasy, science fiction and romance, go to: www.sarinadorie.com

About the Author

As a child, Sarina Dorie dreamed of being an astronaut/archaeologist/fashion designer/illustrator/writer. Later in life, after realizing this might be an unrealistic goal, Sarina went to the Pacific NW College of Art where she earned a degree in illustration. After realizing this might also be an unrealistic goal, she went to Portland State University for a master's in education to pursue the equally cut-throat career of teaching art in the public school system. After years of dedication to art and writing, most of Sarina's dreams have come true; in addition to teaching, she is a writer/artist/ fashion designer/ belly dancer. She has shown her art internationally, sold art to Shimmer Magazine for an interior illustration, and another piece is on the April 2011 cover of Bards and Sages. Sarina has sold over a hundred short stories to markets like Daily Science Fiction, Fantasy and Science Fiction Magazine, and Orson Scott Card's Intergalactic Medicine Show. Sarina's novel, *Silent Moon*, won four contests through various chapter of RWA. It is now published by Soulmate Publishing. Her YA fantasy novel, *Dawn of the Morning Star* out with Wolfsinger Publishing and *Urban Changeling* is available online.

Now, if only Jack Sparrow asks her to marry him, all her dreams will come true.

Information about Sarina Dorie's fantasy novels *Silent Moon, Dawn of the Morningstar, Urban Changeling,* and short stories can also be found at:

http://www.sarinadorie.com

For the latest updates on novels and collections of short stories, please sign up for Sarina Dorie's mailing list from her website or this address below:

http://eepurl.com/4IUhP

A SNEAK PREVIEW OF

Urban Changeling

PROLOGUE
MONSTERS AND MAGIC

My mother always used to say there were no such things as monsters, except for the ones you created. If she'd known what I'd created, she would have screamed. Being a Jehovah's Witness, she would have been horrified to learn I'd been dabbling in magic.

1 CHAPTER
COLLIDING WITH KARMA

It all began with the party. We'd just moved out of Los Angeles because my parents thought the Oregon City School District would be safer. By safer, I suspected they meant quiet, God-fearing, and had students who didn't have sex in the classroom when the teachers stepped out. Which is why my father had found a job in some Podunk town at a construction company belonging to a friend of a friend of a friend. I was thrust into a new school four weeks after the start of the school year.

It was majorly sucktastic.

After a full day of unpacking, my brother Steven and I sat on the back porch listening to music drifting over the trees from someone's yard. The exotic New Age music piqued our curiosity, though neither of us would have dared to admit it. I recognized Enya blasting, and after that, something that might have been Middle Eastern.

Magenta and orange clouds painted the sky in vibrant colors over the tree tops. I sipped my tepid lemonade, the ice having melted an hour before. The air was now cool enough to withstand the humidity in the country air. I lifted my long dark hair from my sweaty neck and held it on top of my head. A gentle breeze tickled plastered strands off my skin. The day had been record heat for September—not the most fun weather if you spent your entire day in an old house unpacking without air conditioning.

My father plopped his sturdy frame down in a lawn chair beside me. "Those hippies and their parties, probably smoking pot out there all night. I thought we would be able to get away from this malarkey when we left the city." He shook his head in exasperation.

My mother followed him out, setting a fresh lemonade beside his newspaper. Her voice came out high and cloying. "Oh, stop! We haven't even met them. They might be perfectly nice people." She patted his bald head. "Tomorrow is Saturday. You know what that means! We'll get to make new friends spreading the truth of Jehovah."

I stifled a moan. Walking door to door doing "service" and passing out *Awake!* and *The Watchtower* magazines did not sound like the best way to make friends. Not that it had ever stopped my mother before. Just once it would be nice to live somewhere people didn't leave flaming bags of poop on your front door because they found your religion annoying. I didn't even know if there would be any other sophomores at Oregon City High School who were Witnesses. Worst case scenario, I would sit alone in the cafeteria during lunch to avoid the worldly people my parents told me it wasn't safe to associate with. Best case scenario, I would find Witnesses who chose not to associate with outsiders . . . just like at my old school. I didn't look forward to either possibility. More than anything, I wanted to find someone like me: a friend who would understand me—and understand what I was going through.

Having nothing better to do other than wallow in the pre-humiliation of the following morning's festivities, I announced, "I'm going to take a walk."

My father shook his head vehemently. "It's nearly nine o'clock. There might be gang members on the streets this time of night. We don't know what this neighborhood is like yet."

My mother laughed, using the cooing voice she used when talking to babies, dogs and my father when he was irritated. "I'm sure it will be safe if Steven goes with her. What do you say, honey? Is it okay for Megan to take a walk if she has her bodyguard?" Out of the two of them, my mother was less strict, but that might have had something to do with her being raised Catholic instead of being born into the religion. My mother ruffled my brother's hair as if expecting him to jump up and volunteer.

Steven and I looked at each other with the kind of loathing only a brother and sister could have for each other. Two years my senior, he was nearly a foot taller and as lanky as a basketball player. Physical education teachers encouraged him to try out for sports. My parents suggested he choose not to join a competitive team for religious reasons. By "choose" what they really meant was, "You will choose what Jehovah would want you to do."

"I suppose I can go if Megan wants," Steven said. He slouched in his lawn chair further, his body language screaming, "Say no! Say you changed your mind about the walk. Don't make me get up."

I stood up.

"Don't stay out late!" Mom said in her syrupy sweet tone. "We have service in the morning."

Lucky me.

* * *

I was drawn to the music like a shopaholic to a Macy's sale. My legs carried me along the shoulder of the road past our quaint stretch of houses and around the bend, only to find the neighborhood streets didn't take me to the cul-de-sac where the music came from. There was no through street. I cut across the field between our row of houses and the neighbors', wading through knee high grass.

"I know where you're going, *peck*," Steven said. "Dad wouldn't approve."

"Don't call me that, jerk wad," I said. "I'm not a hobbit." I wasn't that short, but it was hard not to feel like a midget next to him.

Steven snorted. "It's from *Willow*, not *Lord of the Rings*."

"Like I care."

I waited for him to lecture me on the evils of our worldly neighbors. He didn't plant his heels in the ground and threaten to tattle on me. I suspected he was just as curious as I was. We'd both had more freedom back in the days before my parents had become baptized as Jehovah's Witnesses. Someday, maybe when we were adults, we would make the same commitment and become baptized.

We trudged through thistles and over lumpy terrain, avoiding blackberry bushes along the fence. Flashes of our back porch light shone through the dense growth of trees in our yard. I couldn't see my parents, but I could hear their voices rise high and sharp in argument. I hated the way they pretended everything was all right and denied their problems when the elders asked them about their marriage. Jehovah would know they weren't walking in his truth. He would see how they picked and chose his scriptures instead of following his teachings consistently.

My neighbors singing Kumbaya was a welcome distraction from my parents. In the growing darkness Steven and I became shadows. I pretended my parents and their cutting words were as invisible to me as I was to them.

We snaked through the clusters of dried grass and weeds. Thistles attacked my legs as we crept behind the party house. A wooden fence as high as my brother's head hid the revelry from view. There was definitely the smell of some kind of herb in the air.

"I bet that's marijuana," Steven whispered.

"It smells like cooking spices," I said. It reminded me of Grandma's sage chicken.

The hippie campfire music changed to what I guessed was a recording of a harp. It was pretty, like something I would play on my cello.

Steven spied over the fence and then quickly ducked down. "There are naked people in there."

My religion would blame it on the curiosity of Eve, but I wanted to see.

I found a knothole in the wood and peeped at our neighbors. I was disappointed. They weren't really naked. Women stood in a circle wearing leaf skirts and flower crowns. Most of them wore shirts. A few of the women were topless but their long hair covered their breasts. Little kids laughed and splashed in a kiddie pool off to the side. A table of food awaited the partiers. The aroma of the vegetables on the grill made my mouth water. No one was smoking drugs, but a lady did wave a wand of burning herbs around another woman.

I realized the harp music wasn't a recording when I spotted the girl with golden hair playing the immense instrument in the corner. The party lanterns cast golden lights on her, making her look angelic and unearthly. The airy notes of the music made me feel like I was floating. I closed my eyes and let my body sway to the mesmerizing melody.

Steven elbowed me away from the fence and spied through the hole. "I bet they're lesbians."

"Don't be stupid," I said. "They can't be lesbians. They have long hair."

"Well, they could be Satanic witches."

The harp music ceased. Somewhere in the distance, the irregular rhythm of a drum played. I rounded on my brother. "You would say something like that. You're just like Dad."

"And you're an idealist just like Mom. If I wasn't here, I bet you would ask them to invite you in and they'd sacrifice you, peck."

"Shut up!" I attempted to elbow Steven out of the way to get another glimpse of the harpist but he was as sturdy as an ox.

"No, you shut up," he said. "Hey, do you hear that? They *are* Satan worshippers."

I doubted most Jehovah's Witnesses jumped to the kind of conclusions my brother did. Then again. . . .

I held my breath, listening to the chanting. I couldn't understand what they were saying, but I thought I heard them say something about a moon goddess. I glanced up at the full moon rising over the Douglas firs.

A female voice said from the other side of the fence, "Does our neighborhood's Gladys Kravitz wish to get a better view of the festivities?"

My brother and I both jumped. A pair of twinkling eyes peeked over the top of the wooden fence at us. I was glad for the darkness to hide the panic on my surely red face.

"Er, um, sorry, we were just walking by and curious." My brother backed away. "Sorry, uh, I didn't realize anyone would be naked. Please don't call the police on us."

The head dipped below the fence line. A moment later, a door opened to my right. Light flooded over my brother and me, casting our obscurity to the wind. The harpist stood there, only a few inches taller than me. She must have stood on something before to see over the fence.

I recognized her cream-colored dress as a 1980s Gunne Sax Victorian style that had probably cost a fortune at a vintage boutique. I knew this from my many days of California shopping. The girl's long, crimpy hair was nearly as long as mine, a rarity even among other Witnesses. The golden locks flowed over her slender shoulders, only partly obscuring the fact that she wasn't wearing a bra under the thin muslin gown. My brother stared open-mouthed like a Neanderthal. I elbowed him in the gut. That was what sisters were for, right?

"Hello, I'm Karma Dahl. My mom is hosting a women's

spirituality circle. Would you like to join us?" she asked. "They'll be done with the ritual soon and then we'll have the potluck."

"Oh, um, I don't think our parents would like that. We should be heading back," I said.

Steven stepped forward, his eyes glued on the angel before us. "We could probably stick around for a few minutes longer. Mom won't worry as long as we're together."

The girl laced an arm through mine and guided me over the threshold to the yard. She snapped the door shut behind her before Steven could cross. A wicked grin laced her lips. "Sorry. No boys allowed. This is a women's only retreat."

My heart raced. I would be in so much trouble if I ditched my brother. Plus, they might sacrifice me. The girl seemed nice, but these were worldly people and you never knew what to expect from potential Satan worshippers. And her name was Karma. Wasn't that some kind of pagan word that had to do with bad things happening to people?

My brother rattled the door. His voice rose on the edge of panic, mirroring my own terror. "I have to stay with my sister. I'll get in trouble if I don't. Mom and Dad will worry. They'll call the police if I go home without her. Please!"

Karma put a finger to her lips and inclined her head toward the group of women chanting. "Go around to the front of the house. My brother will let you in."

Steven's feet thrashed through the dried grass.

I noticed the area of fence where she had peeked over contained no furniture or objects she could have stood on. I wouldn't have put levitation past her at that moment.

Karma invited me to make a plate of fresh fruit, grilled vegetables and hummus. She must have noticed my hesitation because she added, "It's all vegan, except for the goat cheese in the tofu gyros that Devon brought. We don't believe in harming other creatures."

I didn't feel comfortable crashing a party and inviting myself to the food, so I declined. I glanced at the circle of leaf-clad women reciting their chant. "So, um, this is a women's music night? It's not a pagan group, or anything, is it? I don't think my parents would be comfortable with me being around witches." Even if they supposedly didn't harm other creatures.

The pagan symbol Karma wore around her neck twinkled in the light of tiki torches like a warning. It looked like a cross with a circle on top. Idol worshippers were not to be trusted.

A wry smile curved Karma's lips upward. She nodded to a middle-aged woman with silver hair. Even if they hadn't had identical builds and hair styles, I would have recognized the resemblance of cherub lips and large, round eyes. "My mom doesn't consider herself a witch. But sometimes I call her that when I'm mad." Her smile grew. "Sometimes I call her way worse things."

I laughed despite this disrespect to her elder, feeling a little more at ease.

Shortly after, her mother padded over with bare feet and bare breasts. I tried not to stare.

"Hello, I'm Octavia. So nice to meet you." Her voice was reedy and distant. I couldn't tell if her heavy-lidded eyes were sultry or sleepy. She didn't cover up her wrinkles with foundation like my mom did.

All this foreignness felt unreal. I was sure if I pinched myself I would wake up.

Karma seated herself at her harp after her mother wandered away. "Do you play any instruments?"

I sat on the grass next to her chair. "I can sort of play the cello, but not very well." Actually, I played very well, but my mother was always telling me not to brag. Humility and modesty were virtues encouraged by the Bible.

As Karma struck up a new song, it drowned out the distant thrumming of a drum. I found myself being pulled into the music. I closed my eyes and swayed in time to the haunting melody.

Karma spoke over her plucking of strings, the sweet soprano of her voice adding to the music. "I plan on being a famous harpist someday. And maybe a social worker. I've always wanted to have a band, but a harp isn't exactly good for rock and roll. You know? It would be fun to play classical music with someone. We could do a duet."

I nodded, unable to speak. I was under her spell and lost in the enchantment of the night.

The beauty of the moon rising above the trees held a power I'd never felt before. There was a quiet electric buzz under my skin, like I was being drawn out of myself. All around me the night was filled with magic. Between the drumming, harp and chanting, my senses felt alive yet relaxed. The lanterns strung across the yard like will-o'-the-wisps illuminated an ornate garden. Children played as happily as cherubs. If someone had told me I had walked into a fairy realm I might have believed them just then. With all my soul I longed for magic to be real. I wanted it so badly my heart ached. And I wanted to believe such things weren't the workings of Satan.

I was so lost in the bewitching world before me that it took me over half an hour to notice my brother still hadn't appeared.

"Where's Steven?" I asked.

"I suppose we could check on him, make sure no one has sacrificed him to any goat god." Karma winked at me.

I didn't laugh at the joke.

As we exited the yard through the back gate and waded through the tall grass, I noticed the thudding staccato. I bit my lip, wondering if something was going on I should be concerned about. Another ritual? With drums. As annoying as my brother was, I didn't want him to be sacrificed to a goat god.

An embarrassed giggle escaped my lips when I found Steven in the driveway shooting hoops. A kid in a wheelchair stole a basketball out of his hands as he dribbled up to the basket. The floodlight illuminated the sheen of sweat on my brother's skin. For being in a wheel chair, the other teenager was giving my brother a run for his money. It was nice I wasn't the only one who had made a friend.

Steven nodded to me as I came into the light. "Hey there, peck."

I ground my teeth. "Don't call me that."

"Sorry to interrupt, Cody," Karma said. "But you know Mom doesn't like you to play basketball in the street after ten. It disturbs the neighbors."

Oh, shoot! It was ten already? My parents would freak. "We have to get home."

My brother halted, staring at Karma. A dreamy look came to his eyes and a dopey grin spread across his face. The boy in the wheelchair took advantage of Steven's dumbfound state to make a basket. He wheeled his chair past Steven to retrieve the ball.

"Hello! I'm talking to you, Cody," Karma said.

He continued to ignore her. My brother continued to drool. Karma turned to me, voicing a sentiment I could relate to. "Ugh! Brothers."

If only Karma had been a Jehovah's Witness I would have felt I'd met my bosom buddy.

2 CHAPTER
DEATH BY HUMILIATION

"Mom, this is too close to our neighborhood," I said. The chill of the morning air seeped through my white sweater and gauzy, flower print dress reserved for religious meetings and ministry work.

My mother powerwalked on the sidewalk beside me, linking an arm through mine to force me to keep up. "Nonsense! This is the territory the Kingdom Hall gave us to spread our truth."

The houses in the neighborhood were a melting pot of eras: nearly identical newer homes sandwiched between old farmhouses and angular 1970s homes. Everyone had a front yard and most of them a back yard. Dogs barked behind fences as we traversed the sidewalk.

The first door my mother knocked on was slammed in our face as soon as she said we were Jehovah's Witnesses. The second house was a cookie-cutter replica of the first. The inhabitants within exclaimed loud enough for us to hear as we approached, "It's the Mormon missionaries. Turn off the television and don't make any noise. They'll go away if we're quiet."

My mom's forced smile strained even tighter across her cheeks as she pretended she hadn't heard.

At the third house, we were greeted by a teenage boy with 666 written in marker on his forehead. My mother gasped and backed away from the door.

Dimples appeared in his cheeks as he grinned. If he hadn't worn so much eyeliner, he might have been cute. I suppose I should have felt more fear at the number of the beast on his forehead, but after the night before, I wasn't sure what constituted devil worship. If I was to believe everything my elders said, long-haired women playing drums were Satanists. Teenagers who idolized rock bands and sported pentagrams and anarchy symbols were going down a path that would lead them from Jehovah's truth.

Sprinklers hissed like serpents along the sidewalk. Maybe I was going down that path, too. My brother and I hadn't exactly volunteered the specifics of where we'd gone on our walk. A nagging worry tugged at my chest. It felt as though a tether attached me to all my sins, the weight of it sinking me farther from heaven and the Lord Jehovah.

I dragged my feet as we neared the next house. The aroma of cinnamon and baking bread wafted out of the windows.

"Why don't you knock on the next door, Megan?" my mother said.

A basketball hoop hung over the garage and a wood fence enclosed the immense yard. I was pretty sure I knew where I was. Of course she would suggest I be the one to knock on this house. Coincidence? Or did she know? Had my brother told her?

My face flushed with heat. "I think I need to, um. . . ." I glanced down at my white dress shoes. There were no laces I could use as an excuse to re-tie. I pretended to stumble a few steps back so that I was in the territory of the yard with the lush lawn. I dropped the bundle of magazines in my arms. Several of them fell into the wet grass where sprinklers were going off.

"Oh, my!" my mother said. "You get that picked up. I'll knock at the next house."

I ducked my chin down so that a dark veil of hair hid my face.

My mother knocked on the door. I glanced up. Cody, the teenager in the wheelchair answered. Relief washed over me. It wasn't Karma.

"Hi, um, are you here for my dad?" he asked.

A wave of homey, baking aromas rolled out of the house. My stomach rumbled even though I'd had a Pop Tart for breakfast.

"Yes, I would love to talk to your parents," Mom said.

"Hey, I know you." He raised his voice. "You're Steven's sister, aren't you?"

I ducked my chin down again and pretended I didn't hear. I turned away and let the sprinklers get me wet, feigning interest in the sopping magazine remaining in the grass.

My mom cleared her throat. "Megan, I think this young man is talking to you."

Knowing there was no way out of this, I stood. I did my best to smile and pretend I wasn't humiliated. Best to get this over with as quickly as possible. "Yes. Nice to see you again. Can I offer you a copy of *The Watchtower*?" On the cover in bold red words was a caption, "Are pagans bad?"

I swallowed. He stared at the words. He didn't take the magazine.

"You two have met? How do you know my daughter?" Mom asked.

"Steven and I met Cody while we were on our walk," I hurriedly supplied. With any luck, he would see my bulging eyes and know the slight shake of my head meant, "Please don't' say anything about the party."

He turned out to be as brainless as my brother.

"Steven and I played basketball. I can't play on varsity in school anymore, so it was awesome to get a little one-one-one action. Where's Steven? It would be fun to play again today."

My mom's smile widened, a genuine expression of joy on her face. "That is so sweet! I'll tell my son to come over later when he's done unpacking."

"Sure," Cody said. "Oh, and I'll get my dad." He left the door open and wheeled backward.

My mother turned to me. She put a hand to her heart. "You and your brother were playing basketball with a crippled boy last night? That is so charitable. Why didn't you tell me that's what took you so long?"

I said through clenched teeth, "Mom, be quiet. They can hear you." I would swear my mom lived to humiliate me.

Seconds later, Karma stood at the door. She wore an old-fashioned nightgown. The embroidered collar and ruffled sleeves resembled something my grandmother would have sewn. Somehow it suited her. It looked far more flattering on her than on Grandma's shriveled frame. She eyed the dripping magazines in my hands.

She flashed a nervous smile. Her words came out hurried. "My mom's still asleep. Why don't you come back later?" She snatched a soggy *Awake!* from my mom and moved to close the door.

"I'm coming!" called a voice shriller than my mom's when she was pretending she wasn't mad at my dad. The door was wrenched out of Karma's hands and a towering woman with shoulder length black hair answered the door. With her potholders in hand and her bric-a-brac trimmed apron, she could have been a Stepford wife. Though I suspected Stepford wives didn't wear crinkly, hippie skirts or bangled bracelets, and show so much cleavage from under their aprons.

Karma frowned at the woman. She didn't look like the lady with long silver hair she'd nodded to the previous night. Her curly hair was glossy black. And she wore a lot of makeup for a hippie. Her black eyelashes were so thick I couldn't believe they were real.

"This is my, um. . . ." Karma paused.

The woman finished for her. "I'm Karma's mother. You must be our new neighbors. It's so nice to meet you. I was hoping to bake a housewarming present for you and drop it off this morning, but apparently it wasn't in the stars. As usual, I overslept. Now here you are." She waved her potholders around as she spoke.

Oddly, I could see a mild resemblance to Karma. Their noses were tapered and delicate and their eyes identically blue. She was pretty in a different way from Karma; a tall regal beauty like a Gypsy queen. Her lips were painted red—my father would have said like a Jezebel.

I'd never seen any woman so beautiful.

Karma's face turned as red as a watermelon. She bit her lip and stared at the floor. When I noticed her "mother's" Adam's apple, I couldn't stop staring. I glanced at my mom to see if she'd caught on.

"That is so sweet of you. I didn't know people did that anymore," my mother said.

"Wait a minute," Karma's "mother" said. "I'm having a vision . . . wait, wait, I can see it in my mind: you're Jehovah's Witnesses, aren't you? Are those *The Watchtower* and *Awake!* pamphlets? That is just so thoughtful of you to bring them. My brother's family are Witnesses. May I take an extra for a friend? By the way, honey, those pink roses on your dress are lovely. Karma, would you fetch that bread? It's vegan. Dairy-free and egg-free and you wouldn't even know it."

Karma sighed as if in resignation. It looked like she may have been as embarrassed by her father—mother?—as I was by mine. I gave her a reassuring smile as she backed away.

Karma's mom pulled off a potholder and extended her hand. The long, tapered fingertips were painted red. "Oh, where are my manners? I'm Zelena. I'm a spiritual midwife." She shook my mom's hand. "Would you care to come in for some tea, darling? I can read the leaves too. You might like what they have to say." She winked.

"No, thank you." An artificial smile materialized on my mom's face. "We don't believe in soothsaying."

Zelena leaned in close, her shrill voice lowering to a whisper. "Yes, yes. By the way, he's not really mad at you, honey. He's mad at himself and he has too much pride to be the first one to apologize. Not that you have to listen to my advice, but if you asked him to go with you to counseling again, he'll say yes this time."

My mom gasped and pulled away.

On the top of my mom's stack of *Awake!* magazines was one with the headline: "Shouldn't we love all our neighbors?" Oddly, I didn't remember *The Watchtower* having a caption that said, "Peace, love, rainbows and tolerance," either, but maybe I was mistaken.

3 CHAPTER
WELCOME TO HICKSVILLE

At the Kingdom Hall, I sat through the recitation and prayers, studying the people around me. I tried to pick out the other teenagers my age but they all looked too old or too young. Afterward, my parents were greeted by other members.

A lady in a pink pastel dress introduced herself to my mom. "It's nice to finally meet you after all the emails, Sister Johnson." She must have been the lady who had told my mom about the job for my dad. We'd been thanking Jehovah for her helpfulness every night.

"This is my daughter, Felicity," she said, indicating a girl my age in pigtails. "It would be lovely to have you over for the women's Bible study at our house sometime."

From the short length of Felicity's hair and the sheen of tinted lip gloss on her lips, I suspected her parents weren't as strict as mine.

My dad shook hands with Felicity's father, all smiles and fake happy eyes like he always did when in public. He droned on about how he had been raised as a Witness but strayed away during his "hellion years" only to come back to the flock for the sake of his children. I tried not to yawn.

Felicity stared, enraptured by his story. It probably was interesting to those who hadn't heard it a bazillion times.

"How long have you been in the truth?" Felicity asked.

My dad squeezed me to his side, something he only did in public. "We've always raised our children with strong values Jehovah would approve of."

"Four years," I said.

His back went rigid. "Ten."

My mom inserted herself back into the conversation. "Oh, no, more like twelve."

I didn't think you could count all those years my mom and dad had tried fifty different churches, or argued about which religion Steven and I should be raised. But hey, what did I know.

I met the other Jehovah's Witnesses who were close to my age. The boys were either in middle school or college. The two who had graduated the year before were prim and polite in the way Witness boys often were to girls. Then again, maybe it was because they were older. They weren't exactly welcoming to Steven.

"How nice," Felicity said. "Now there will be four of us. No one will be the third wheel." She twirled a brown pigtail around her finger. "Do you like horses?"

"I'm pretty sure I'm allergic." If my sinuses couldn't handle cats, dogs, cows or rabbits, I doubted any other furry creatures would be tolerable.

Gail came up and joined her friend. She could have been her clone, with her matching dress and youthful pigtails, except that her complexion was darker. Beth joined us last. She was the only one with biblically long hair. Like me.

"I'll show you around school tomorrow," Beth said. "We're the only ones there." The only Jehovah's Witnesses, she meant. "Do you like horses? You should come riding with us tomorrow."

"Um. . . ." I said.

"Yay! You're going to come riding with us!" Felicity said.

The three girls joined hands and circled around me like they were five instead of fifteen. I told myself that if Job had endured, so could I.

4 CHAPTER
DAY ONE IN HIGH SCHOOL HELL

Since I didn't want to share a locker, I was assigned a half locker in the senior wing. It was upstairs on the other side of the school where I didn't even have classes. Within the first day someone wrote in permanent marker: "Go back to the Witness protection program." The next day someone crossed off "Witness" and rewrote "Witless." It was an improvement from Mission High School in Los Angeles. Someone had peed in my locker on the second day.

The downside? I couldn't get the marker to come off. People laughed and pointed every time I went to get my books. One of the teachers even yelled at me because he thought I had written on my own locker. Craptastic. The office said they would ask maintenance to remove it with some special cleaner.

Karma invited me to sit beside her in Biology 1 and Beginning Orchestra. She wore white bloomers under another white vintage dress. I suspected that was the only color she owned. During lunch I sat with Gail, Felicity and Beth on the stairs near the gym. Karma walked down the stairs where we ate, offering me a small smile. She didn't invite me to join her. But maybe that was because of the group of boys drooling over her everywhere she went. Mostly they were boys with eyeliner, crazy colors of hair and multiple facial piercings. I suspected they were Satan worshipers. It made me sad knowing these were her friends.

Beth leaned toward me conspiratorially. "She's someone to stay away from."

"Why?" I set my turkey and cheese sandwich down on my pink lunch box.

"Can't you tell from the crowd she hangs out with? She's a devil worshipper. She'll curse you if she gets mad at you. Plus, she'll cast a spell on any boy you like and make him fall in love with her."

I picked up my sandwich and continued eating. "I'm not allowed to date, so it doesn't matter. Do your parents let *you* date?" I glanced at Karma caught up in her swarm of admirers. One of the boys left his open locker to talk to her. She stared over her shoulder at me.

I offered a little wave. Her gaze swept over Beth and she turned away.

Beth snorted. "That's not the point. And do you see all that makeup she's wearing? And the way she's almost hanging out of her dress. My parents call her a whore of Babylon."

"Um. . . ." I had no idea what to say. My parents would never say that about anyone. "It doesn't look like she's wearing any makeup to me."

Felicity held her tinted lip gloss poised in front of her mouth. She discreetly capped it and tucked it next to her hip. "A little bit of makeup isn't a sin. We have to make our own choices about what is right for ourselves."

Gail slurped on her juice box. She and Gail both wore T-shirts with horses on them and Wrangler jeans.

Beth crumpled her Capri Sun and wadded up her fruit snack wrapper. As she sauntered over to the garbage can at the end of the hall, Gail leaned forward and whispered, "Beth isn't always like this. Just when her cousin does something to make her mad."

Karma? Her cousin? No way. They didn't act related either.

"Plus, Karma is weird." Felicity said. "She used to be Goth and wore all black. Now she only wears white. Her mom is a nudist hippie and her dad had a mid-life crisis and now thinks he's a woman. I don't know why his wife didn't divorce him."

"Wow, that's really. . . ." I struggled for the right word. Cross-dressing was probably a sin, even if he was still married to the same woman. On the other hand, it was admirable a married couple would work together to survive something like that. I wondered what it would be like to be loved by someone so unconditionally they would accept you even if you did make a drastic change to your lifestyle. I doubted my parents would even last the year. They'd been getting counseling from one of the elders at our old Kingdom Hall. They'd stopped going, though, because whenever they came home from their sessions they fought even worse.

I told my brother about Karma and Cody's parents as we walked home from school together. With our house only a mile and a half away, it took us less time to walk than to wait for the bus. Plus, buses were full of barbarian bullies.

"I hung out with Cody at lunch," Steven said. "We played basketball in the gym for a while, but some teacher blew his whistle at us and said we had to stop because Cody could hurt people if he accidentally runs over someone's foot."

I stared out at the dusty field across the street where horses grazed. "I guess that makes sense. His wheelchair could break someone's toes."

"He's run over my foot twice already. It doesn't hurt much worse than a two hundred and fifty pound dude stepping on my foot. That teacher was an idiot."

I raised my voice to be heard over the cars passing us. "Maybe the teacher is afraid Cody's chair will get knocked over and he'll get hurt."

"Whatever. I told Cody I thought he should talk to his mom about it because she's a lawyer and she should get on that school's case."

I wondered if he meant the biological mom or the he-mom.

"But Cody won't cuz he doesn't want to make a big deal about it." He clenched and unclenched his fists at his side. "It just makes me so mad."

My brother rarely got this riled up over anything—except when we fought over the remote. "Why don't you start with a petition or something?"

"That might not be a lame idea, peck."

I smiled. That was the closest I ever got to a compliment from my brother.

"Speaking of things that don't suck. . . ." A dreamy look came across my brother's face. "Did you see Karma today?"

A rusty blue car drove by, veering closer to the shoulder so we had to dodge into the ditch. Teenagers screamed inside as they threw something at us. I raised my arms to shield my face as the splatter hit. A tin can smacked my brother square in the chest. The chunks reeked like fishy cat food. Nausea washed over me.

This was still an improvement from Los Angeles. It could have been scalding coffee.

Steven looked down at his shirt and then back at the car speeding off. "Did you see that? It was a 1961 Camaro."

As usual, my brother had his priorities in the wrong place.

5 CHAPTER
DAY THREE AT MY NEW SCHOOL: REAL MAGIC

"Are you in 4H?" Gail asked. "It would be so fun if you came."

I leaned against the row of lockers where we sat eating in the hallway. Lunch was my favorite period of the day. Aside from orchestra.

"Um, don't you have to have an animal for that?" Hello allergies.

Felicity picked a hair out of her sandwich. She kept pulling and pulling. It was Rapunzel length. The grossest thing about it was that she had short hair, so it made me wonder whose it was. She offered, "You could come to the barn with us and ride my horse after school."

Yeah, I could also punch myself in the face for no reason.

Felicity and Gail were perfectly nice girls, even if they did wear T-shirts with horses on them every day . . . and every topic they discussed revolved around horses. They ate, drank and dreamed of horses. It wasn't bad hanging out with them without Beth, who was sick that day, but it wasn't . . . well, it just wasn't special. It wasn't the bosom buddy relationship like *Anne of Green Gables* had with Diana—like what I had felt that night with Karma.

Karma even made biology class fun. Or I suspected it was her that made it fun. I wasn't sure who else could have been behind the frog resurrection.

Biology was fifth period the following day. The entire science wing smelled like formaldehyde. Between the heat in the school and the lunch I'd just eaten, going into that classroom made me want to barf. There were all these pictures of dissected animals on the walls. At my old school we'd still been covering the basics and looking at cells. But this teacher wanted us to have some "fun" to see what biology was all about early on. And as everyone knows, frog dissection is buckets and buckets of fun.

Karma sat beside me at the black lab table. She wore a lacy dress from the eighties that might have been someone's wedding dress. I had never cared for ruffles and puff sleeves, but after seeing them on Karma, they grew on me. I lined up our tools as the teacher droned on. When it came time to retrieve frogs from the bin up front, Karma raised her hand. "My religion doesn't permit me to eat meat or harm living creatures. I can't participate in this activity."

I admired her courage. It gave me a panic attack to tell the teacher it was against my religion to say the Pledge of Allegiance, or that I couldn't participate in class parties if there was a holiday theme. I had learned in L.A. it was better not to speak out.

Mr. Burton grimaced over his spectacles. "Then you can take notes as your lab partner dissects. If you choose not to do that, you can get an F on the lab. Your choice."

Karma collected the frog from the bin next to the teacher's desk. She cradled the limp creature to her chest as a child might hold a teddy bear.

"It's okay, sweetie," she cooed. "I won't let the big, bad teacher hurt you."

One of the girls at the front of the classroom waved her hand frantically. "Mr. Burton! Are you sure these frogs are dead?"

"Of course they are. I ordered them from—"

Ribbit.

Snickers sounded from the students all around me.

Mr. Burton put his fists on his meaty hips. "Very funny. I will have you know—"

Ribbit.

This ribbit was closer. It sounded pretty real.

"Dude, my frog just moved," a boy with a cowboy hat said in the back.

A girl screamed, followed by another. *Ribbit, ribbit, ribbit.* A frog jumped out of the plastic bin and landed on Mr. Burton's computer. The frogs in the classroom came to life, wiggling and hopping almost as much as the screaming students around them. In the chaos of students running from the room, and some running in from surrounding classrooms, Karma calmly walked over to the window and slid it open. Her frog jumped free.

Her lips curved upward in a wicked grin. "I guess we don't need to worry about dissecting after all."

"Wait. How. . . ? Did you. . . ?" I stammered.

"Magic."

Please visit Sarina Dorie's website for information on how to purchase Urban Changeling.
www.sarinadorie.com

Made in the USA
Middletown, DE
06 June 2016